SHIFT

SHIFT

A Novel

Matt Brown

To order additional copies of this book, contact:
Xlibris Corporation
1-888-795-4274
www.Xlibris.com
Orders@Xlibris.com

40086

That a man's eyes may wander is not a mystery. Nor is it, by itself, reason for concern. But when his eyes are turned away from the right things for long enough, it is his soul that will wander. And though this drift away may occur effortlessly and unconsciously, the journey back often requires great effort, resolve, and courage.

1

Edmonton, Alberta. 1:00 a.m.

Although they were on the road, the two men were recognizable to all in the Whyte Avenue pub. Kevin Wilkins and Billy Morrison were two thirds of the top Vancouver Canucks line. A few disgruntled Edmonton fans still lingered, sporting their Oiler jerseys and beer-dampened scowls after the visiting team's upset win. One of the patrons bravely uttered a parting sentiment on his way out the door.

"Canucks suck!"

The two players smiled. They were out later than their coach would have liked. But they had a day off before their game in Calgary so their leash was long. A winning coach is a happy coach.

"Another tap-in for Shenks tonight. He'll break fifty goals without taking a hit, thanks to us," Kevin speculated. His linemate looked him in the eyes inquisitively then asked him a question he knew the answer to.

"What is it with you and him?"

"What do you mean?" Kevin answered evasively.

"How come every goal he scores is another thorn in your side?"

Kevin scrunched his brow and responded, "Doesn't it get to you that we do all the dirty work and he's the media darling? The fuckin' Canuck poster boy?"

"Nope."

"No?"

"No," Billy repeated emphatically. "All I know is I'm playing on the top line; I'm at a career high in points; I'm on a team that's finally fucking playoff bound; and I'm a plus nineteen going into my option year. Due in large part to that Canuck poster boy," he added, crossing his arms. Then he smiled and shoved his friend playfully.

"You're fuckin' hopeless, Wilkins."

"What?" Kevin objected.

"Your fuckin' glass is full and you're bitter that Koshenko has more foam than you."

Wilkins looked straight ahead, his poorly fought half-smile acknowledging the point.

"Boo-fucking-hoo," Billy teased.

"Why do I even talk to you, Morrison?"

"I keep you in check, bro. You need me," Billy closed with a laugh.

Two attractive women eyed the men from the end of the bar. Kevin and Billy returned the glance.

"I wonder if Erin's awake," Kevin mumbled uneasily, noting the time difference in his head. His eyes continued to hover around the ladies whose interest in them was decreasingly subtle.

"Wilk," Billy prompted.

"What?"

"I'm not your fuckin' Jiminy Cricket," Billy said with a smirk.

"What?" Kevin replied, looking puzzled.

"In thirty seconds, when those chicks come over here, you'll have to be your own guardian angel, brother, 'cause I've got the morning off. I'm on the prowl, baby."

"You want another beer?" Kevin asked, avoiding the subject.

"That's my boy, Wilk! Another round for the fellas!" Billy said grandly, tussling his buddy's hair. Thirty seconds was a good guess.

2

Los Angeles, California. 9:43 p.m.

Kevin looked up at the clock from the visitor's bench. Game tied, 3-3. Just under three minutes left on the clock.

Head Coach Marcel Boucher called from behind the bench, "Wilk, Mo, Shenks, next shift."

"Let's go boys!" Wilkins yelled instinctively from his seat. "Strong finish now!" The L.A. forwards controlled the puck in the Vancouver zone. Back to the point. A shot through traffic . . . and a loud ricochet off the post. While the crowd let out a collective groan, Vancouver captain,

Rick Olsen, corralled the puck and chipped it off the glass and out of the zone. As the L.A. defenseman retreated to pick up the puck, the Vancouver forwards changed. The Canucks' top line jumped onto the ice. Morrison took the angle on the L.A. forward advancing the puck, he batted a flip pass out of the air. Canucks' defenseman, Kyle Kopp quickly controlled the bouncing puck and slapped it up the middle to the centreman, Koshenko. Fighting off the hook of the L.A. defender, Koshenko flipped a backhand pass to Wilkins, streaking down the right side. With a step on the other defenseman, Wilkins pulled the puck hard to his backhand and flipped it up over the goalie's shoulder into the top left-hand corner. The Crowd moaned.

As the Canucks celebrated the goal, Kevin Wilkins thought silently to himself, *two more for forty. That'd be big*. Affirmation rang over the P.A.: "Canucks fourth goal scored by number twenty-nine, Kevin Wilkins, his thirty-eighth of the season. The assists to Vladimir Koshenko and Kyle Kopp. Time of the goal: 17: 43 of the third period."

L.A won the face-off. They gained the red line and dumped it in. The L.A. goaltender raced to the bench for the extra attacker. On the Vancouver bench "Olse, your line get ready." Rick Olsen nodded. The Vancouver defenseman slapped the puck around the boards. The bouncing puck was mishandled by the L.A. player and Koshenko picked up the puck near centre. Wilkins again hussled to open ice. "Shenks!" he yelled for the pass. But Koskenko had room and slid the puck surely into the empty net. *Nice one, Shenks!* Wilkins thought. *Can't have another 40-goal man on the team, eh?* Wilkins reluctantly touched gloves with his linemate to congratulate him.

The last minute and a half passed uneventfully. The Buzzer sounded to end the game.As the team walked down the tunnel, Billy Morrison led the cheering' "Woo! Fuckin' rights, boys! We're going to the play-offs!" An L.A. media director touched Wilkins and Koshenko on the shoulder. "Three stars, fellas. Then Sportsnet wants to grab you for an interview, Kevin." "No problem," Wilkins replied.

He'd done more and more interviews as the year had worn on and his scoring pace picked up. At twenty-five, this was a breakthrough season for him. He reflected as the camera crew adjusted for the shot. Finally he was getting the recognition he felt he deserved. Twenty-five and twenty-seven goals were respectable in his two prior seasons, but they didn't get him much attention. Now he had passed through his 'up-and-comer' status, and was on the verge of stardom.

"I'm here with Canucks' forward, Kevin Wilkins. Kevin, it must have been a great feeling to get the winner in an important game like this one."

"Yeah, Billy got some good pressure and forced the turnover, then Vlad did the work to set it up. All I had to do was finish."

"And a nice finish at that. You looked a little disappointed after the empty-netter by Koshenko. Were you hoping for number thirty-nine?"

Kevin was shaking his head before the reporter could finish. "Naw, I was just relieved that we sealed the win. These games down the stretch are too important to worry about numbers. There'll be time enough for countin' at season's end." Kevin smiled and winked into the Camera. "Hey Tory, Daddy's home in a few days."

"Alright, thanks Kevin. Kevin Wilkins with the game-winner as the Canucks clinch a play-off spot and will go to the post season for the first time in five years. Back up to you, Ray".

After showering and changing, Kevin made his way through the media to the pay phones in the corridor. Their next stop was Phoenix. He had a call to make.

"Hello Chelsey?"

"Hey rock star, I saw the game. You were awesome!"

"Thanks. We fly in tonight, then play the day after tomorrow. I'd like to see you."

Rick Olsen walked out of the locker room and saw Kevin on the phone. "That Erin, Wilk?" Kevin covered the receiver and looked at Rick, saying nothing. Knowing it wasn't Kevin's wife, Erin, Rick's look turned cold. He should have known it wasn't Erin. He'd have used his cell phone. He looked away for a moment, feeling reluctant to say what he felt, then looked back at Kevin, with his eyes narrowing in disgust. "Tell her I say hi," he offered sarcastically and kept walking.

Rick and his wife, Kate, had become close to Kevin and Erin during Erin's pregnancy, four years earlier. They provided a lot of support for both of them, since the pregnancy was a difficult one. Rick, now thirty-three, had taken Kevin under his wing. He had come to think of him as a little brother, a sentiment that Kevin liked.

But things had deteriorated between Kevin and Erin, and Kevin now sought more and more affection outside of his marriage. There's no shortage of opportunities for 'affection' for the professional athlete, especially one of Wilkins' stature. Earlier in his career, the six-foot-two, muscular Wilkins had shrugged off the advances of young women seeking his attention. But now he found this harder to do. And in a few cities, he sought out the same women again on return visits.

Rick knew and did not approve, but he was torn between two roles. As a friend, and a husband and father to a family of his own, he wanted to put an end to it. He wanted to confront Kevin. He had begun to feel awkward around Erin, guilty with the secret. She was his friend too. She too was like a younger sibling. But he was also a teammate. And teammates know and abide by one simple rule, with no exceptions; what happens on the road stays on the road. Even though most players frowned upon the 'wine & diners' who slept around habitually, the unwritten code took precedence. Rick walked to the bus, feeling heavy with knowledge he wished he'd never acquired. He sat down and took out his own phone. He wanted to hear a voice that would take him away from this place in his head.

"Kate? Hi Sweetie."

"Hi Hun. How was your game? You guys win?"

"Yeah, we're in the play-offs."

"Oh awesome, good for you!"

"Yeah, thanks, it's pretty exciting. How are the girls?"

"They miss their daddy." Rick laughed gently, then sighed heavily.

"Rick, you okay, Honey?" Kate had a way of reading his mood, even on the phone.

"What? No, no, I'm . . . I'm good. Just . . . I'm just tired. . . . I miss you."

3

Vancouver. 11 p.m.

Erin Wilkins stood in the doorway of her daughter's bedroom, watching her sleep. She smiled and tilted her head slightly sideways as she watched. But there was a sadness in her smile. An uneasiness. She longed for her young family to be as perfect as she had dreamed it would be. As perfect as it seemed to be a couple years earlier. But the vision of her angel sleeping blurred with tears and gave way to the memory of an argument that she and Kevin had had a week ago. She'd kept her feelings to herself for longer than she could stand. But now that the problem had been brought out in the open, she wished it hadn't. She was afraid. Afraid of losing her husband. Afraid of losing her daughter's father. The uncertainty was overwhelming.

She wanted to go back to pretending that nothing was wrong. It was an illusion, but at least it felt safe. Her head went over their exchange, over and over.

"What do you mean, 'something's changed', Erin?"

"I don't know, you seem different. You seem distant."

"Since when?"

"Since . . . just . . . gradually, over the past couple of years."

"And now you bring it up?"

"Kevin . . . You're not the man that I married! Now you're all about the money and the fame and 'oh, look at me, I'm in the all-star game, I must really be something now!' And all I can think about is what you're not anymore."

"Oh, and what's that?"

"You used to play the game because you loved to play . . . We used to stay up late and talk for hours because we didn't want the nights to end . . . You used to tell me that everything else came second to *us* . . . You used to talk to me about everything . . . And now I can't get two words out of you that don't have to do with hockey."

"I used to be a kid, Erin! Look around you! The only reason we have all of this is because of what I've become!"

"I don't want all this! I want you! The real you!"

"I can't talk about this right now. I'll call you from San Jose."

Kevin had called from San Jose but the conversation was short and, of course, about hockey. But Erin wasn't distressed about what they talked about, but rather what they didn't. She bore her soul to him. She finally told him what she saw slipping away from him, and he responded flatly . . . and he hadn't brought it up since.

She walked down the hall to the bedroom. It was nice and big when Kevin was home. It was too big when he was not. She combed out her auburn pony tail, sitting on the bed. She was petite but still athletic looking. She felt she owed Kevin the work it took to look pretty. The players wives didn't compete to look the best, but they were all aware of how the others looked. No one wanted to be the one that 'let herself go'. She used to take comfort in the notion that Kevin saw more in her than good looks. She wasn't sure anymore. Worse yet, she wasn't sure if she was even pretty to him anymore.

The phone rang. *That's him*, she thought. She ran to the dresser where she'd left the cordless, then paused. *Maybe I can say something to make things okay again. Maybe he'll say something.* She took a deep breath as she hoped.

"Hello?"

"Hey Erin."

"Hi Kev. I saw the game. You were great!"

"Thanks. Did Tory see?"

"No, she missed it. She was in bed already . . . sorry."

"Oh well."

"I'll tell her about it in the morning. She'll think that's neat."

"Yeah."

"Kev . . . I really miss you, honey."

"Miss you too. Listen Erin, sorry to cut this short but I'm supposed to do a couple interviews for the papers here."

"Um . . . okay . . . then I guess I'll talk to you when you get to Phoenix."

"Sure, bye for now."

"Bye, Kev."

Erin set the phone down, closed her eyes, and let out another deep breath. Another day to wonder what would come of their relationship. Another day to search her memory for the turning point in their marriage. She'd heard about marriages being changed by a child, when the attention required to care for a baby took away from the intimacy that a couple shared. But that wasn't it. Tory, if anything, was their greatest source of intimacy. Caring for Tory brought them even closer together. They saw in each other a tenderness that they both were attracted to. They both loved being a family, a tight little unit against the world. They were once in love with each other and experienced that love even more through caring for their child. Now Tory may have been the only real connection between them.

Watching Kevin with Tory gave Erin hope that she could rescue that part of him that she had fallen in love with. It was her best and only indication that he could still love wholly and unconditionally, that he could still play and laugh spontaneously, at no one's expense, with no bottom line. The child in her was strangely jealous at times that Tory could still bring that out in him, while she could not. But for now it was what she held onto. A wink at his daughter on T.V.

But the heart of the matter was still unsettled. Tomorrow she would regain her courage to believe in their marriage. But tonight she would grieve what she feared was lost. The phone call had settled nothing. Had she known it was the second one he had made after the game, perhaps her will would have been broken. But instead, Erin curled up on the bed and began to sob, biting her lip to keep from waking Tory, simultaneously hoping for the best, and fearing the worst.

4

Dallas. Three nights later. Second intermission.

Kevin sat in the locker room, still shaking his head at the scoring opportunities he'd failed to cash in on. He'd been held scoreless the night before, in Phoenix. Rick had the only goal tonight, a short-handed goal to pull them within two. Kevin had hit two posts off of highlight reel plays by Koshenko, but the score remained 3-1.

Coach Boucher had been into the room with a couple of strategic adjustments, and now stood out in the hall, conferring with the assistant coaches. Rick Olsen now held the attention of the players. "Let's be patient out there, fellas. There's lots of time. Just keep pressuring the puck and take what they give us." Billy barked an addition to Rick's instructions in his own trademark fashion, "Let's put the body on their fuckin' D-men boys! They're gettin' tired!"

Some players sat forward and nodded with each instruction. Others sat back and waited quietly, reflecting on their own role in the third. Vlad Koshenko sat retaping his stick methodically, less out of necessity than superstition. Kevin sat staring off into space. Chewing slowly on a Powerbar, his thoughts wandered. He anticipated the awkwardness of his return home. He'd spent the night with Chelsey in Phoenix and replayed his brief phone conversation with Erin in his head from earlier in the day.

"We'll be back late. I'll try not to wake you coming in."

"That wouldn't be so bad, Kev. I haven't seen you in a week; I could stand to be woken." There was a hint of uneasy laughter in her voice.

"Well, we're off tomorrow. Maybe we could take Tory to the park or something."

"Sounds nice. Listen, Kev, . . . I've been feeling really off since our talk before you left. I just . . . I want to work this . . ." her voice cracked and she paused, taking a deep breathe to regain her composure. Then she forced out all that she could say, in barely more than a whisper, "I love you, honey".

"Love you too. See you when I get back."

As he played it back in his head, he was disturbed by his flatness of emotion. Rather than feeling eager to reconcile, he felt annoyed that he had one more thing to deal with when he got home. He was ashamed of himself for allowing images of the 19 year-old Chelsey to occupy his mind while he had talked to his wife. Erin had given him all that he had ever asked, and he had somehow lost interest in her. *What kind of guy does that?*

For Christ sake, Kev. Get it out of your head! You've got a game to play! The players made their way through the tunnel to the bench for the third period. Billy slapped Kevin's shoulder pads with both gloves and looked him in the eyes, "Show time, brother! Let's rock and roll!" Kevin smiled and gave a single nod of agreement, trying to quiet his mind as he walked.

Dallas carried the play for the first half of the period, but the Vancouver goalie, Mark Dorsey held the Canucks in, keeping the score at 3-1. Billy drove a Dallas forward into the boards, knocking him off the puck in the neutral zone. He fired a crisp pass to Kevin heading up ice. Kevin bobbled the pass with his stick, losing it into his skates. He quickly kicked it up to his stick and *Crack!* Kevin didn't see the Dallas defender, all-star blueliner Chuck Madison, coming the other way. What he saw now was the ceiling of Reunion Arena, it's lights blurry and spinning. He saw a foggy number five skating back into the play, and heard the crowd still buzzing from the thunderous hit. Kevin struggled to his feet and glided to the bench, still groggy, thankful that the hit happened so close the visitor's bench.

Canuck's head trainer, Tony Paxton, pulled him aside to examine him. The fog lifted as Paxton conducted a series of quick tests. "He's alright, Bouche. He'll be ready to go next shift." Boucher nodded, then glanced at Kevin, "Keep your head up, kid, or Madison will take it right off next time."

Kevin sat uncomfortably with a sick feeling in his stomach, feeling shaken from head to toe, wondering if there'd be any major damage when the adrenaline wore off. He looked straight ahead, pretending not to hear the jeering of fans leaning over the glass, "Welcome to Dallas, punk!", "That's licence plate # 5, Wilkins!" Original as always, but more embarrassing than usual.

When Kevin finally refocused on what was happening on the ice, the Canucks had possession in the Dallas zone. The third line was working well in the corners, controlling the puck, then sending it back to Kopp at the blueline. Matteus Krohn, the feisty little winger drew two defenders going to the net. Kopp faked the long shot and hit the other winger, Conrad Soles, with a pass at the side of the net that Soles directed into the goal. 3-2.

Four minutes to play. Morrison stripped defenseman, Madison of the puck on his way out of the zone, spinning and shooting. The goalie made a pad save but the speedy Koshenko tapped in the rebound to make it 3-3. Kevin tallied Koshenko's totals automatically in his head. *That's 47. Another easy goal.* The frustrated Chuck Madison shoved Kevin from the crease, where he stood over the Dallas goaltender. Kevin caught his heal on the post, tumbling to the ice. Kevin jumped to his feet, again embarrassed by the Dallas defender, and with both hands, thrust his stick into the face of Madison. Madison, who had looked away, didn't see it coming and crumbled to the ice. Another Dallas player pulled Kevin to the ice from behind and a swarm of sweaters from both teams converged on the pile. Beneath the pile, Kevin saw the stream of blood dripping from Madison's mouth. He was sickened by what he had done.

Once all the players were separated, Kevin was assessed a five-minute major penalty and a game misconduct for high-sticking. He walked down the tunnel to the Canucks' locker room, his head hanging, and eyes glassy like a deer in the headlights. As he walked, he searched his mind for what had come over him. A bad game is one thing, a cowardly act like that was completely inexcusable. Never in his career had he attacked another player so viciously, without mutual engagement in the conflict. Madison had lightly shoved him away from the goalie, as much out of reflex as frustration. His response? A stick in the mouth, with all of his strength. Out of embarrassment. Out of shame. Out of rage. Then from back down the tunnel, Kevin heard the siren. Dallas had taken the lead.

Now overwhelmed with more emotions than he could count, he broke his stick against the wall, "Fuck me!" Media representatives scattered as he threw his helmet down the hallway on his way into the room. He dropped himself down on the bench like a 6-year old who just finished a tantrum and buried his head in his hands. The media would have a field day with this, and he knew it. Moments later the siren blew again. 5-3. And yet again one more time, 6-3. Then finally the buzzer. The game was over. Now he had to face his teammates.

As the players walked past him in the room, Kevin could feel their eyes on him but didn't dare look up. Hockey's a rough game, and people get hurt, but there are unspoken 'rules of engagement' that he had broken. Strange as it may sound to an outsider, if two players look each other in the eye in order to consent to a fight, then otherwise brutal acts of violence are considered to be part of the game. But when the assault comes in the form that this one did, few players on either side will see it as anything short of cowardly.

Billy Morrison sat down in the spot next to Kevin, but didn't start to undress. He leaned forward and stared straight ahead. Kevin knew what he was going to ask.

"So what the hell happened out there?" Billy asked, turning his head towards Kevin but not looking directly at him.

"I don't know . . . I . . . I just snapped, I guess." A weak reply, but all he could come up with.

"No shit." Billy retorted, with a half laugh laced with sarcasm. "Fuck, Wilk. I wouldn't have expected you to blow a gasket like that in a million years. That was . . . oh, hell, I'll just say it. That was brutal." He shook his head and added again, "Brutal." One of the things that Kevin liked about Billy was his honesty. You never had to wonder what he was thinking. But at this moment, it was making a difficult moment worse, especially since Billy was right on the money, and they both knew it. There was no point in defending what he'd done. "I know, Billy. I don't know what to tell you."

Billy glanced up at Kevin then away again, then got up and walked to the Powerade dispenser. He usually didn't do that until his shoulder pads were off and he'd talked to his buddy, Wilk, about the game for a couple of minutes. But they were done talking for the night.

Then a voice from the door. "Wilk." It was Jamie Harris, the assistant coach that everyone called 'Bones' but no one knew why. "Bouche wants to see you when you're changed."

When Kevin walked into the coaches room, they were watching a tape of his crosscheck on Madison. Boucher let it play, rewound, let it play, rewound, then advanced the tape frame by frame. Kevin glanced up at the screen through the corner of his eye, hoping that it wouldn't look as bad as it had felt. But through the miracle of television, it actually looked worse. Chuck Madison turning his head away, still disappointed by his miscue, obviously not expecting that shoving a player from the crease would warrant retaliation. Then frame by frame, Kevin jumping to his feet and throwing all 220 pounds of his frame into a crosscheck in the face of one of the most highly respected players in the league. The tape didn't show the blood pouring from Madison's mouth, because of the scrum that ensued. But Kevin still saw it in his mind as he watched the tape, as it had been burnt into his memory, as if with a branding iron.

Coach Boucher paused the tape, took off his glasses and rubbed his eyes with his thumb and index finger. "There'll be a suspension Wilk, and a fine. On the heels of the Zholtik hit, we'll just have to hope there are no criminal charges laid". (There had been an incident a few weeks earlier in which New York defenseman Alexander Zholtik had delivered a two-handed tomahawk swing over the head of Florida tough guy, Marc Sevigne. A criminal investigation had led to charges being laid. Sevigne was still recovering from head and neck injuries.) Kevin nodded, staring blankly at the floor.

"I talked to Roger a few minutes ago (Roger Parsons, the General Manager). He wants to be proactive on this to minimize the damage."

Kevin finally looked up. "What does that mean?" he asked, looking confused.

"Well, we need to give them some reason why you might not have been of sound mind. Are you having any personal problems, Wilk?"

Kevin looked up at the ceiling and turned away, "oh, you've got to be kidding me," his voice drenched in disbelief.

Bones spoke up "Wilk, you screwed up, buddy. We're trying to find a way to make this go away quickly".

Kevin trusted Bones but didn't like where this was going. But he was emotionally exhausted and no longer had the energy to fight it. He turned and stepped towards the door, then stopped, looked over his shoulder and spoke, "Say what you have to say. I'll go along."

Tony Paxton met him in the doorway and directed him back in with a hand on his shoulder. "Well, I've got some pretty good news," Paxton said, addressing the whole room. "I talked to their trainer. We went to school together at UBC. Madison has a pretty nasty cut in his gums, under his upper lip, but that's basically it. No teeth out, no fracture, no concussion . . . or not a bad one anyway."

Wilk wondered to himself, *Exactly what constitutes a good concussion?*

"They've stitched him up and he won't likely miss any time." He turned to Kevin, "An inch lower and he'd have been spittin' chicklets."

No one in the room was in the mood for colourful analogies. "Thanks Pax", Boucher said to close the discussion.

"You up to facing the media, Kevin?"

"Not really."

"Alright, I'll talk to them."

5

Vancouver. A few minutes later.

Erin sat on the couch, her feet tucked under her body, just having watched the television broadcast of the game. She was still in shock at what she had witnessed. The station was going to another program, so she turned to TSN to see if more would be said. They were going to a live press conference with Marcel Boucher.

"I'll fill you all in as best I can, but then I have to get to the airport.

"We are relieved to hear that Chuck Madison's injury is not as serious as it could have been. Kevin Wilkins is deeply apologetic and will attempt to convey that personally to Chuck as soon as he has the opportunity. Unfortunately, Kevin is going through some personal difficulties that may have resulted in his volatile behaviour." The crowd of media began to buzz. "The Canucks' organization is going to ensure that he receives the counselling that he needs to resolve whatever difficulties he is experiencing."

Erin felt her heart drop into her stomach. For a moment, she felt on display, like the whole world was now privy to her problems with her husband. But then she turned her focus to Kevin. *Obviously he's been in turmoil. This outburst was completely out of character. Did I provoke this? Did I push him too hard before he left? What if he wondered if I'd even be here when he got home? If Tory would be here?*

The phone rang.

"Kev?"

"Um, no Erin it's Kate. I was just wondering if you were okay."

"Yeah, I'm okay."

"Well, my mom is here visiting and doesn't mind watching the kids, if you'd like some company."

Erin, like Rick, could conceal little from Kate. At that moment she felt like Kate could see inside her, that she knew that she was in pain. As she searched for the words to convince Kate she'd be fine, her emotions bubbled to the surface. Her eyes welled up, and after a moment of fighting it, Erin started to sob.

"I'm coming over, Erin. Okay?"

Between sobs, Erin squeaked out a barely audible "okay".

Kate had talked to Rick minutes before. Rick explained why the story had been spun as personal problems for the press, and more importantly, for league officials. But Rick also knew that Erin had a tendency to worry on behalf of others and suggested that Kate call and see if she was all right. But Kate knew there was more to this than a hit after the whistle. *Erin sounded much more than worried. She sounded desperately distressed, like she'd been pushed over the edge. This event may have pushed her over, but why was she so close to the edge in the first place?* As Kate drove across town to Erin and Kevin's house, she caught herself presuming. *Stop trying to figure it out, Kate. Just go there and be with her. She'll tell you if she wants to.*

When Erin came to the door, her eyes looked red and sore. The skin under her nose looked chafed, like she been blowing it constantly for days. Kate couldn't hide the concern on her face. Erin's state far exceeded her expectations. The look in Kate's eyes set Erin off again, and as she started to cry, Kate grabbed her and pulled her in, pulling Erin's head in under her chin.

"It's okay, dear. Just let it out."

"This is so stupid. I can't stop crying."

"It's not stupid, Erin. Whatever this is, it's got to run its course. Fighting it will only prolong it."

After a minute or so, Erin looked up at her friend. Her mouth curled up into a faint smile, "Thanks, Kate. You're the best." Kate smiled back, took both of Erin's hands, and asked, "Feel like talking about it?" Erin nodded emphatically, "Sure. Keeping it to myself hasn't done me any good. I'll put on a kettle."

Erin and Kate sat for two hours talking. Erin told her everything. She told her about the loss of closeness from their relationship. She told her about Kevin's obsession with his scoring totals, newspaper articles, endorsements, and anything else he could tie to his 'superstar status'. She explained how sick she was of complaints about his linemate, Vlad Koshenko.

Erin explained the things she missed the most. Simple little things. Cuddling first thing in the morning. Flirting around the house, like high school kids. Talking about places they wanted to go in the off-season. Reminiscing about the 'old times' when they started to date in Saskatoon, while Kevin was playing junior.

Erin had been assigned to Kevin as a peer math tutor. She never thought she'd date a hockey player. Lord knows she'd been warned by enough people not to. But she saw something different in Kevin. A tenderness. She saw depth in his personality. He seemed reflective and intelligent. He was this great guy who also happened to play hockey. Plus her family dog loved him immediately, which scored him 'serious points' because "that dog wouldn't let most boys through the door".

Erin talked about the times when she'd be over to his place to help him with his math. "We actually *did* math! We'd sit close to each other, not touching, but so close that when he grazed me, I'd get goose bumps and a tingle down my spine. And he was so sweet. He admitted, once we were dating, that he hadn't wanted to make a move and make things awkward if I wasn't interested. He said that he'd been out with other girls but could never respect them. They called them puck bunnies. None of the players took them very seriously. But he said that I was special, and that he felt like so much more than a hockey player when he was with me. I think that's the sweetest thing that a guy had ever said to me. I think that's when I really started to fall in love with him."

Erin talked about Kevin's proposal, walking along the river in Saskatoon. She talked about their honeymoon in Florida, and even pulled out photo albums. Some find other people's wedding albums boring. Not Kate. She was thrilled. Besides, the shot of Kevin in mouse ears was well worth the trouble. Erin talked about how thrilled she was for Kevin as his playing career gained steam. Both Erin and Kate reminisced about Tory's birth, and how cute Kevin was, bouncing around the hospital ward while it was going on. In particular, Erin remembered the look of adoration that Kevin had as he sat with mother and child.

Kate sat and listened, smiling and nodding. As she listened, she heard Erin's voice change. It became more lively and hopeful. She talked more and more about what she loved about him, rather than what upset her. Kate saw Erin's energy rebuilding. It clearly had been depleted over the past few days.

Kate listened as Erin told her what part she thought she might have played in setting Kevin off in Dallas, then she countered.

"Erin . . . I hear what you're saying, but I just sat here and listened to you talk about what you guys have had in the past. You brought up what you're feeling because you want to restore that, not because you wanted to hurt him. You're fighting for your marriage and all that you know it can be. You're fighting for him. He said it himself; He feels like more than a hockey player when he's with you! You're trying to give that back to him. Don't give up."

Erin took a deep breath and nodded, looking Kate right in the eyes.

"Thanks, Kate. This was great medicine."

"It was a good talk wasn't it?"

"Mm hm, much needed."

"You gonna be okay if I go?" Kate touched the side of Erin's cheek, like she did her own children.

Erin squeezed her hand and nodded, "I'll be fine."

6

On a plane. Somewhere between Dallas and Vancouver.

Kevin sat restlessly, mulling over the events that had transpired. *They actually want me to see a counsellor. Unbelievable.* Coach Boucher had informed him before they got on the plane that Roger Parsons had insisted they follow through with their statement that they would send him to a counsellor. Failure to follow up, if it were ever discovered, might upset league officials who would construe the original statement as a hollow attempt to influence a disciplinary decision. In any case, what Kevin thought about the idea was hardly relevant. He was feeling too sheepish to challenge the decision.

As he grew more tired, Kevin's thoughts became less specific, shifting to scattered images of the Dallas game, Chelsey in Phoenix, Erin and Tory in Vancouver, and an assortment of other random images that seemed unrelated. Eventually even these images faded, leaving only a general sense of malaise. Life didn't feel right to Kevin. Lately he felt like he was living someone else's life, one that didn't fit his soul, like that feeling when you've slipped your right foot into your left shoe. Hockey felt like a job, not a game. One that he now used to prove himself, not simply to play, like it had once been. His encounters with other women made him feel more and more lonely, like eating chocolate when your body yearns for real sustenance. Each compulsive act of infidelity pushed him further and further from Erin. He used to feel so close to her that he could tell her anything. Now he was constantly having to sort out what he'd really been doing from what he had told Erin, the exhausting maintenance of two different worlds. He had grown quieter around her, paralyzed by the fear of slipping up and revealing a discrepancy.

At the same time, Kevin had watched Rick, his surrogate big brother, push away from him. But Kevin didn't blame him for this. He'd taken on a lifestyle completely at odds with Rick's. Kevin glanced over at him, a couple aisles away. He was asleep. His face looked unburdened, content to be heading home. Kevin wondered what dreams coloured Rick's sleep. Satisfaction from a job well done? He'd led a struggling team to its first play-off in years. Thoughts of his soul mate, Kate? Visions of his three children running to the door?

Then the face of Kevin's young daughter, Tory, took shape in his mind. She was so curious and energetic, mindful of others, cuddly at ever opportunity . . . all things he had loved about Erin. She was playful and light-hearted, but determined when she focused in on something, traits he felt she took from him. Loyal . . . a former trait of his. He let go of the thoughts of what he'd lost in himself and settled in on Tory, the one blessing that nothing could obscure. He pushed his head into a pillow against the window, and finally drifted off to sleep.

The jolt of the runway woke him with a start. He had actually been sleeping for an hour but felt like he'd just dozed off. As the plane rolled to the gate, Kevin found himself a little more at ease, surprising considering the aftermath that would surely come from the Dallas 'incident'. He felt like he'd torn his sights from a focus that was wrong for him. The result was a panicked uneasiness until he refocused on priorities closer to his heart. It was like that sensation when you realize you've been following the wrong person through a crowd. First you wonder how long you were following the wrong person, as you scan the crowd frantically for the person you're with. Then when you spot them, you see you've got some catching up to do, at least they're in your sights.

Rick came and stood beside him while they waited for their bags.

"We off tomorrow, Olse?"

"Yep, no meetings, no workout, no skate."

"Maybe we could get the kids together . . . go to the park or something?"

Rick looked at Kevin, pleasantly confused by the offer. Kevin tried to identify the look on Rick's weary but smiling face. *Maybe forgiveness? Maybe not.* Rick put his hand on Kevin's shoulder and gave it a gentle squeeze. "Good call. I'll suggest it to Kate in the morning."

7

Kevin walked quietly into the house, careful not to wake Erin or Tory. He locked up and dragged himself up the stairs. It had been a long road trip. Only a week, but certainly eventful. He stopped at the doorway of Tory's room. The sight of her warmed him like a blanket as he leaned against the door frame. Then he walked down the hall to the master bedroom. Erin lay curled up on her side of the bed. She always left his spot vacant, even during road trips. *Tory looks just like her mom when she's sleeping*, he thought.

He undressed to his boxers and slipped under the covers. He lay transfixed by his wife's sleeping face, like he was looking at her for the first time. Delicate, fine features, but with faint lines of experience and wisdom. Her hair straight and shiny from the night light in the hall. She smelt of apricots. She'd obviously showered before bed. Kevin leaned over and kissed her softly on the cheek. Her eyes opened, slightly surprised at first, then narrowing as she smiled, "hi sweetie".

"Hi . . . sorry, I didn't mean to wake you."

They gazed at each other for a moment, then Kevin asked, "why so smiley?"

"I've just been thinking a lot about you . . . about us. Kate was over tonight. We had a great talk."

"Yeah? What about?"

"Lots'a stuff. Mostly reminiscing. It helped me to remember all the good stuff about you . . . about us."

Kevin smiled shyly. He felt like he'd been given credit for a goal he didn't score. "Seen any of that stuff lately?" He winced after he asked, wishing he hadn't.

"Well . . . I think I've been looking for the things I didn't like lately." Fair enough. As diplomatic a response as he could have hoped for.

"You see the game tonight?"

Erin's face changed to one of concern. She pushed up onto her elbow, "yeah . . . what happened?"

"I just lost it. I wasn't myself all game. He'd embarrassed me once earlier with a big hit."

"I saw that too. It looked like it hurt."

"Yeah, but my pride more than anything. Anyway, I just had a whole mess of bad stuff in my head when he pushed me over in the crease and . . . well, there's no excuse for what happened."

Erin was quiet. She agreed. Silence for a moment.

"They're making me see a counsellor."

"I know, Rick told Kate . . . Well, maybe that's not such a bad thing. You said you haven't been feeling yourself." Erin instantly felt bad for suggesting it, but Kevin didn't look offended.

"Yeah, but what am I going to say to someone I don't even know?"

Erin shrugged, still thinking it was a pretty good idea.

"You know who I should talk to? . . . Cormie."

"That's a really good idea, Kev."

"That's what I'm gonna do. I'll call him in the morning."

Gord McCormack, affectionately known as 'Cormie' by his players, coached Kevin in major junior in Saskatoon. He had been like a father to Kevin when he was in junior. Kevin's father had left his mother a few weeks after Kevin left for Saskatoon. He hadn't wanted to upset Kevin until he was "settled" with his junior town. Kevin's relationship with his father subsequently deteriorated. At the same time, Kevin's hard work and determination won him a place in Cormie's heart. Gord McCormack became Kevin's number one supporter, and apart from Erin's entrance on the scene, his best friend.

Both Kevin and Erin were content with the idea. Erin leaned over and kissed Kevin on the lips, "Good night, sweet prince." She giggled as she nestled up against his shoulder.

"Good night, Wilk," Kevin responded with a smile. That was the pet name she inherited after their wedding. She hadn't heard it in a long time.

8

Kevin woke to the sound of tiny feet sprinting down the hall. As he opened his eyes, he saw the 3 ½ year-old Tory launch herself onto the bed, "Daddy!!!" She wrapped her arms around him like a vice. Kevin reached over his shoulder to Tory's head of chestnut hair and ruffled it playfully with his hand. Tory tightened her grip. Erin walked back into the bedroom from the ensuite, smiling widely at her husband and child. As she passed the bed, Kevin reached around her waist and tugged her easily onto the bed. Erin let out a tiny scream of surprise, then laughed as Kevin wrestled her under his arm. Tory's giggles turned to high-pitched screams of pure glee. Kevin hugged his two girls into his chest, feeling truly safe for the first time in as long as he could remember.

Kevin and Erin's eyes met. In Erin's eyes, Kevin saw a warmth that can only be described as maternal, that look of pure contentment when a woman catches a snapshot of her happy family. She resolved at that moment that she would never allow what they had to fall into question again. What they shared was too special. Kevin kissed both girls on the forehead.

"Why are you crying, Mommy?" Tory inquired. Erin didn't realize she had welled up.

"I'm just really happy, sweetheart." Tory was confused but content with her response, then shifted her attention.

"Let's watch cartoons on your T.V., Daddy."

"Sure, L. Dub." (L.W. was short for Little Wilk.)

Kevin sat up against the head board. Tory bounced to her spot under his arm. When he flicked on the T.V. with the remote, TSN was showing highlights of his game the night before. Kevin was stirred back to reality immediately, almost having forgotten the events that had unfolded in Dallas. They were on Rick's short-handed goal, before the incident. He felt a shudder of panic, not wanting Tory to see what had happened. Erin felt Kevin's sudden tension, and put her hand on his shoulder for support. He quickly turned to YTV, the sure bet for some cartoons. The channel change was quick enough for Tory not to realize her daddy's team was on the highlights. She quickly lost herself in the program.

"Actually, L Dub, watch with Mommy. Daddy's got to make some calls."

"Okay, Daddy." Tory replied, her eyes still glued to the television.

Kevin got up and grabbed the cordless off of the dresser. They had slept late enough that some of the league disciplinary action would be underway. It was time to face the events from the night before. But he felt strangely at ease with it, having renewed his resources with his family. He also felt less overwhelmed since his decision to enlist the help of an old friend.

Kevin dialed Jamie Harris' direct number. He knew that Boucher would be there early too, but felt much more comfortable talking to Harris.

"Jamie Harris."

"Bones, it's Wilk."

"Hey Wilk. Thought it might be you. Haven't heard anything from the league office yet."

"Actually, Bones, I was hoping you could do me a favour." Kevin felt sheepish asking a favour under the circumstances, but also knew that Bones was his best bet. "Did you ever meet Gord McCormack, my coach in Sask?"

"Only briefly. I played and coached against him. Why?"

"Well, I've been thinking about this counsellor thing, and he's the closest I've had to that. I'm not sure it would do me any good to talk to someone I don't know. Anyway, I was hoping that I could get in touch with him instead of a counsellor."

"Well, it sounds like an okay idea to me, but it's not really my call. If you hold on for a second, I'll run it by Bouche."

"Sure."

Harris' office was right next to Boucher's. Kevin could faintly hear them talking but couldn't make out what they were saying. He was surprised at how nervous he was, waiting for an answer.

"Wilk?"

"Yeah."

"He says that's fine, but if anyone asks, you're seeing a counsellor, not an old coach."

"No problem. Thanks, Bones. I owe you one."

Harris laughed. "One?!"

"Okay, maybe a few more than that." Kevin was relieved to hear Bones laugh. It made him feel a little more confident that things might return to normal.

"I'll give you a call when I hear something, Wilk. Are you going to be at home?"

"Um . . . call my cell. We might take Tory to the park."

"Will do. Say hi to Erin. I'll talk to you soon."

"Yep, later Bones."

When Kevin flipped to Gord McCormack's number in his book, he saw the Saskatoon number that had been crossed out, a number that he still knew by heart since he'd called it so frequently years before. The new number was for a Calgary address. Cormie was semi-retired, having taken an assistant coaching job with the major junior team in Calgary. He wanted to be closer to his mother, who passed away only months after his arrival in the city.

Kevin paced in the hallway as he awaited Cormie's voice. "Hello?"

"Lornie! It's Wilk." The players in Saskatoon had nicknamed Lorna McCormick 'Lornie'. She liked that she'd been given a name like 'one of the boys'.

"Well hello, Kevin! How are you?"

"Um, actually I've been better." Kevin hid nothing from Lorna. He knew she'd probe if she detected anything. She was the 'mother hen' wherever McCormack coached.

"I kind of lost my cool on the ice and I'm probably facing a suspension."

"Oh dear," Lorna replied with a sigh.

"Yeah, the worst part is I deserve it. Is Cormie around?"

Lorna paused then answered awkwardly, "Gord's at the hospital, Kevin. I'm afraid he's very sick."

"Sick?" Kevin prompted reluctantly. He tried to prepare himself for the answer. Lorna paused again. "It's cancer, dear."

Kevin's chest tightened. His own problems dissolved in his head, while his body took on a whole new feeling. One of profound despair. "Is it . . . I mean, is he gonna . . . he's gonna be okay, right?"

"They don't know yet, Kevin." Lorna had been fighting her own fears about her husband's condition for several months. At this moment, her concern was for Kevin. She knew he shared a close bond with Gord, and felt unable to protect him from the truth.

"Oh, Gord will be so thrilled that you called, Kevin. Shall I have him give you a call back? I'm on my way over there. I can tell him right away."

Kevin replied instinctively, "I'm coming to see him. Can I do that?"

Ordinarily, Lorna would ensure that he was not going to too much trouble, and insist that he could just phone instead. But she was past that point. She knew that Gord's condition was not good. She hoped that seeing Kevin might make a difference.

"Oh, Kevin . . . he would like that very much. Let me know when you're coming in. I'll come and get you."

"I'll rent a car. Don't worry about it. Where is he?" "He's at the Tom Baker Centre at the Foothills Hospital. Do you know where that is?"

Kevin answered before she finished asking. "I'll find it. I'll be there today." Kevin paused for a moment, with a question sitting uncomfortably on the tip of his tongue. "Lorna . . . why didn't he call me?"

"He didn't want to trouble you, Kevin. I told him you'd want to know, but . . . well you know how he is."

Kevin did know. He had never met anyone as selfless as Cormie. "Yeah, I know. I'll see you later, Lornie."

"Alright, dear. This is very sweet of you. Bye for now."

Erin had watched from the bedroom, unable to hear the conversation. But she could tell that there was something wrong. She hadn't seen this look on Kevin's face since the complications of her pregnancy.

"Kev? What's the matter, honey?"

Kevin leaned back against the wall, staring blankly at the wall in front of him. He drew his head back, closed his eyes, and slowly let out a deep breath. Then he looked Erin in the eyes, "Cormie has cancer."

Erin's brow wrinkled with concern. "Oh God. Is it . . ."

"They don't know. I'm going to see him."

"I'll come with you."

"I'll be fine, Erin."

"I'm coming with you, Kevin."

"What about Tory?" Kevin asked, still expressionless and glassy-eyed.

"Maybe Kate will take her. I'll figure something out."

Erin took Kevin's hand, looked up at him and took a breath, as if about to speak. She was searching for words to take his distress away. When none could be found, she pulled herself close to him, resting her head on his chest. She knew that there were times when only a hug could help, times when people needed to feel things, but could at least feel less alone in feeling them.

9

As Kevin and Erin pulled away from the Olsens' house, Tory waved from the window, flanked by the Olsen girls. She was thrilled to stay with the Olsens, whose three daughters, modelling the example of their mother, spoiled her with attention. Kevin and Erin knew she'd be in good hands while they were gone.

Kevin's cell phone beeped. He checked the incoming number as he drove. It was Bones. Kevin had all but forgotten the events of the night before, and barely acknowledged them in his mind as he answered.

"Hey, Bones. What's the word?"

"Five games. Five grand in fines. Sorry, Wilk. Tough timing. That takes us three games into the play-offs."

"Well, . . . it is what it is. No point getting in a twist over it. I'm on my way to the airport. I'm going to see Gord McCormack in Calgary." Kevin didn't think Harris needed to know why.

"That's good. If anyone sees you going, it'll look like you've been sent to a specialist or something . . . helps the cover."

Kevin rolled his eyes, bothered a little by the insincerity of the whole pretense. He just wanted to be off the phone. "Thanks, Bones. I'll call you from there."

"Okay, try to get some rest, buddy. You sound tired."

"Alright."

Kevin turned off his phone and glanced at Erin's inquiring expression. "Five games, five thousand dollars." Erin saw no protest in his face. She knew his thoughts were elsewhere, and gently rubbed his thigh.

Nothing was said on the way to the airport or while they waited to board. Erin was waiting, hoping that Kevin would eventually let out some of what was on his mind. She had started to lose hope until after they had taken off. She was watching the ground shrink below when he finally spoke.

"Lots of people beat cancer. Cormie's got such a great attitude, he'll beat this for sure."

Erin knew that a positive attitude affects cancer prognosis. Her mother, a nurse, often talked about its importance. But her mother had also told stories of exceptions. People with terrible attitudes surviving the disease, courageous patients losing the battle. She couldn't bring herself to confirm his guarantee. "He's definitely got a great attitude." It was the best she could do, knowing what she knew.

"It might not even be that serious. Lornie said they didn't know. I think I've been assuming the worst."

Erin couldn't respond. She knew he had started to protect himself from the idea of Cormie dying. He obviously needed to back away from the idea. It was too uncomfortable. But he was also right. They didn't know. They'd just have to wait and see. But Erin also recognized a familiar pattern that made her uncomfortable. Kevin never seemed to face his feelings head on. When he felt something uncomfortable, he had a tendency to either talk himself out of it or distract himself from it in some way. He rarely allowed himself to feel anything but the good things.

She thought back to the night before when she finally let herself feel her own fear, her own hurt, and how relieved she felt when she had faced it. She wondered how many things still boiled beneath the surface in her husband. How heavy must it be never to give oneself the license to feel openly?

Kevin's mind escaped to his junior years in Saskatoon. One game resonated in his mind as the best summary of what Cormie was all about. Down 3-1 in a play-off series to Swift Current, the Blades found themselves trailing 2-0 after the first period. The whole team was tight, like they were trying *not* to make mistakes, trying *not* to lose. Cormie stood at the doorway of the room, watching the players file in, trying to sense their mood, assessing what they needed from him. What followed was painted like a portrait in Kevin's mind. Cormie walked slowly into the centre of the room and began to talk.

"Lots of scouts out there, hey boys? Sure, it'd be nice to impress them in a big game like this one. But here's the thing, fellas, and listen up, because this is really important. We all want to move on to the next round. We all want to impress the scouts. We all want to improve our stock. But we've forgotten the most important thing: *playing the game.* You go ask any player in the NHL when he had the most fun playing hockey. What you do think he'd say?

Kevin spoke, barely audibly, "junior hockey."

"You're God Damn right . . . junior hockey. You're sitting in a room with twenty young guys full of piss and wind . . . full of life, about to go out and test yourselves against twenty other guys who are just as talented, who want it just as bad. But right now, we're wasting the experience. It's all about where we want to go . . . who we want to be. Well, do yourselves a favour. Let go of that for the next forty minutes, and just *feel* the game. What does it feel like to move the puck? What does it feel like in the corners, when the adrenaline's pumping? What does it feel like to depend on nineteen other guys? What does it feel like to break up a two on one? To handle the puck? To drive full speed to the net? Right now we're not feeling any of it . . . because our heads are somewhere else. If you go out there right now and just play the game, and experience it for what it is . . . a game . . . then I promise that where you're going will take care of itself. And as for who you want to be? Well, let me save you the suspense . . . you're always going to be you. And you can either accept it and enjoy it, or waste your time wishing you were someone else. So what do you say, boys?" His mouth drew up into a smile. "Ready to play some hockey?"

The room erupted. "Fuckin' rights, boys!" one player agreed. "Woo! Let's get it on, brothers!" from another.

Kevin's best descriptor of the next two periods was "magical". To this day, he could not remember a more passionate performance from a whole team. They were unburdened by the outcome, in spite of its importance. They played physically, intelligently, and unselfishly. The scouts scribbled frantically in their notebooks, but that didn't matter. Most of the players had forgotten that they were even there.

And what made it more special was the response from Swift Current. The opposing players rose their level to match that of the inspired Saskatoon squad. The result was poetry on ice; forty young men played the game of their lives. Four thousand fans were treated to the fastest, hardest hitting contest that they had ever witnessed. The building was electric. Kevin assisted on the Blades' second goal, knocking a Swift Current defenseman off the puck in the corner, and rifling a pass to the front of the net where it was directed in by a pinching defenseman. He then scored the equalizer with under three minutes to play, on a deflected point shot.

When Swift Current scored the overtime winner, the crowd erupted, and stayed on its feet applauding the efforts of both teams. In the locker room, the mood was unusual. The players were both devastated by the loss and immensely proud of themselves and each other. Players hugged, cried, . . . and smiled. The looks on their faces shared, without words, a feeling that they'd been a part of something special. Something no one could ever take away. On the sports page, it was a 4-3 overtime loss, eliminating the Blades in only five games. But to the players, it was a pinnacle. An experience of the game in its purest form.

Kevin broke out of his trance to see Erin's inquisitive look. "Thinking about the Saskatoon days?" she asked.

"Yeah. Good guess." Although he wasn't surprised that she knew. She seemed to have a knack for pinning down his thoughts contextually.

"Is Cormie the best coach that you've ever played for?" Erin asked, trying to keep Kevin talking.

"Well, I've definitely had better technical coaches . . . you know, the X's and O's of the game? But Cormie made it fun. He loves the game and it rubs off on people. He's the kind of coach that you want to play hard for. Not because you're afraid not to, but because he's so thrilled when you do. If you're happy, he's happy. And he'd take a bullet for any one of his players . . . Put it this way, Cormie's the best *person* I've ever played for."

Erin smiled and squeezed Kevin's arm. She loved when Kevin was sentimental. Once in a while he'd say something that revealed his depth, his vulnerability, . . . his humanity.

Kevin's smile faded as he gazed straight ahead. "I hope he's gonna be okay," he said softly.

Erin nodded, inhaling deeply. "Yeah . . . me too."

10

Tom Baker Cancer Centre.

Gord McCormack leaned over the bathroom sink, looking at his reflection in the mirror. His eyes were dark and heavy. His young friend, Kevin Wilkins would soon arrive. He wished his appearance wasn't so discouraging. Gord sighed deeply, "You don't look so good, Cormie" he mumbled to himself. The words got partially caught in his throat and he began to cough. It was a deep, thick cough, drawn fully from his lungs. He looked down at his hand that he used to cover his mouth. His palm was barely visible beneath the dark layer of clotted blood. He rinsed off his hand and spit out the rest, rinsing the metallic taste from his palate.

He'd been hospitalized once again as a precaution for the heavy bleeding in his lungs. In two days, he would go into surgery for the second time, hoping that they would be able to remove all of the cancer this time. Although he tried to stay upbeat, the idea of chemotherapy again was almost more than he could stand. As a player, he lived with pain everyday. It was part of the game. But that pain was manageable and short-lived. He could not have imagined the agony that the chemical treatments would inflict on his body. Long sustained pain, the feeling that his whole body was so polluted that the cancer couldn't possibly survive. But somehow it did, and he was about to go through it all again.

And this time, it was even worse. In the x-ray, his lungs looked like they were stuffed with cotton. "Carcinoma of a very aggressive nature" was how the doctor had described it. As a coach, he'd always liked the word 'aggressive'. In this context he found it less appealing.

"Gord? You okay in there?" Lorna probed from outside the door. "I'm . . . I'm fine."

Gord always knew that Lorna had a strength about her, but the last several months had revealed a strength of monumental proportions. Her insistence that he would survive cancer had been unwavering. She had held onto hope at the darkest, most discouraging moments in the process. When he couldn't sleep, she was up with him. When he cried, she held him. When he doubted, she reassured him. When he slept, she prayed for him.

He had long since stopped trying to protect her from the reality of his situation. She was up for the fight, even when he was not. She had lost two parents to cancer, many years before, but somehow had not been broken by the struggle. He'd had a quote from Friedrich Nietzsche up in the Saskatoon locker room, "That which does not kill you, makes you stronger." It was true of Lorna. He hoped it would be true of him as well.

The voices from the hall suddenly registered as two that he knew. Kevin and Erin were asking about his whereabouts at the nursing station. Lorna followed him out into the hall. "Wilk!" Gord's energy quickly rose as Kevin turned to see him.

"Hey! Cormie!" Kevin smiled widely as he walked over. He wrapped his arms around his friend. Gord felt frail to him, a condition he had never associated with his old coach. Kevin was stirred back to reality by the obvious signs of the disease.

Gord grabbed Kevin by both arms, leaned back and looked at him. "It's great to see you, Kev."

"You too. Let's go sit." Kevin directed him back towards the room.

"Glad you could come too, Erin." Gord said, turning to acknowledge her.

"Me too, Gord. Hi Lorna, good to see you." Erin smiled warmly at her old friend.

"We're so thrilled that you kids could come." Lorna exclaimed, pressing her hands together.

"So Cormie, Lornie says you've got a battle to fight here," Kevin prompted, not wanting to say 'cancer'. His face barely held a smile.

Gord nodded slowly, trying not to appear beaten. "Yeah, I suppose I do. You guys kept warning me about the smokes, didn't you?"

Kevin shrugged, not sure how to respond.

"Well, why don't you and I go get some coffee, Erin, so these two can catch up . . . uh, unless you're up for some hockey fish tales." Lorna laughed knowingly.

"Coffee it is!" Erin replied playfully.

Gord and Kevin followed them to the doorway. The two women made their way down the hall.

"Now how old is little Tory?" Lorna asked directing her full attention to Erin.

Erin waved to Kevin, then turned to Lorna and began chatting. Kevin turned to Gord as the voices faded down the hall.

"We both lucked out in the wife department, didn't we Wilk?" Gord said, still watching down the hall.

"Yeah, . . . How'd they do?" Kevin asked jokingly.

Gord laughed aloud, but then his laugh triggered another coughing fit. Kevin shuddered when he saw the blood, even though it was much less than the cough just prior to his arrival.

"You okay, Cormie? Should I get the nurse?" Kevin's tone was nearing panic.

"Not much they can do, kid," Gord responded soberly. "I'm okay." He wiped his hand with a tissue, quickly changing the subject. "So what the heck happened in Dallas?"

"You saw that, huh?" Kevin replied. "Ah, Cormie . . . it's been over a year since we last talked hasn't it?" he added, not quite sure where to start.

Gord tilted his head back, as if checking a calendar on the ceiling, "Wow, yeah, I guess it has," he replied, realizing that the rest of the world kept moving during his first bout with cancer.

"A lot has happened since then." Kevin said, really meaning 'we have lots to talk about'.

Ordinarily, the two would talk for an hour on the phone before they were done 'talking hockey'. But something was different now, as if the salience of Gord's condition lent urgency to their reaching the 'heart of the matter'.

Kevin stared out the window blankly, then slowly shook his head. "I've made some pretty messed up choices in the last little while, Cormie."

"Alright, kid", Gord gestured towards himself with his hands, "out with it."

Kevin finally had a chance to bear his soul, so he took it; "I cheated on Erin."

Gord closed his eyes and hung his head, "ah geez, Kevin," he muttered quietly. He very rarely called him Kevin. "Does she know?"

"No. If she did, I think she'd have left me by now."

"How did it happen?"

"Well, for a long time, she just seemed to be losing interest in me. But instead of asking her about it, I just felt sorry for myself. The next thing you know, you've got a few drinks in you, you're telling your life story to some skank on the road and 'boom', you're past the point of no return." Kevin didn't see any point in editing his account.

"Well, . . . obviously it was a dumb-ass thing to do, Kev, but what started your relationship downhill in the first place?" Gord matched his candor.

Kevin shrugged and shook his head, "I don't know."

"Oh, come on, Kev. Think back." Gord leaned forward, disappointed with the news, but engaged in the idea of helping instead of being helped.

"Well, she said something fairly recently about me changing. But that was just a week or so ago."

"Maybe she just finally said it. How did she say you had changed?"

"I think basically she thought that success was going to my head, and I was too focused on stats and stuff."

"So are you?" Gord pressed.

Kevin felt under fire, and paused, contemplating whether he was willing to keep talking about it. He looked Gord in the eyes. He had forgotten momentarily whom he was talking to. But then he felt his defenses drop, confident that Cormie wouldn't ask unless it was his intention to help. He saw the vulnerability in Gord's condition and, taking a deep breath, accepted his own.

"It sucks you in, Cormie. You get a taste of stardom and you forget about the things that used to mean everything to you. You put enough pucks behind the goalie and everyone starts to treat you differently. And it feels awesome! You feel like you're on top of the world! But then something happens. You see how quickly it can be taken away. You see, there's only so much attention to go around. And once you've had a taste, . . . well it's pretty addictive."

"Betcha can't eat just one?" Gord added, trying to ease the tension.

"Exactly!" Kevin laughed, surprised he had it in him. "Anyway, you start comparing yourself to other players. Who's got more goals? Who's making more money? Who's in the friggin' Doritos commercial?" Kevin laughed again, this time at himself.

"Is the game still fun to you?" Gord inquired purposefully.

Kevin paused, then responded shamefully, "It's fun when I score."

"You believed the hype, Wilk."

Kevin looked up, awaiting an explanation.

"Remember that stupid rap CD you guys used to play in the room . . . you know, with the guy yelling 'don't believe the hype! Don't—don't—don't believe the hype'" Cormie bobbed his head mockingly.

"Right. Public Enemy," Kevin recalled, laughing.

"Well, I thought that was pretty good advice. I see it all the time, even in junior. Kids get a taste of success and they let it go to their heads. But here's the thing, Wilk. If you believe that success makes you better than anyone else, then what happens when you fail?"

"Well, you're probably going to be a miserable guy to be around." Kevin answered, following the logic.

"Right. And how about if you're successful?"

Kevin shrugged.

"Well, you'll probably be just as hard to be around, because you're putting yourself above everyone else, right?" Gord continued, helping Kevin along. Kevin smiled and nodded, astonished at how simple Cormie could make it all seem.

"Now I'm not a very religious guy, but someone told me once that the Bible says 'pride comes before the fall', and I think that's bang on. You start tying your worth to a scoring title and you'll either end up an asshole or a basket case." Gord said emphatically, wondering if he'd pushed too hard.

"Or in my case, both." Kevin laughed, relieved that he could admit it to someone.

"So what are you gonna do about it, Kev?" Gord asked, hoping that Kevin could see his way out.

"I don't know, Cormie. It seems like the damage is done. It may be too late." Kevin shrugged, resigning hope.

"Ah Christ, Wilk! Bite your tongue! You're gonna sit here in *my* hospital room telling me about *too late*?!" Gord barked.

Gord's point was well-taken. Kevin shrunk down in his chair, embarrassed that it had to be made out loud.

"Look, Kev, who are the people giving you all the attention right now?" Gord pressed on.

"The fans, the media, . . . groupies, if you want to call them that." Kevin was again right with him in his line of thought.

"And tell me this; you walk away from the sport right now, will any of those people give a crap about you?"

Kevin shook his head.

"Well you've got a wife that would love you if you were . . . pumpin' gas, and I'm betting your little daughter doesn't need a Hart trophy to love you."

Kevin smiled, warmed by the thought of Tory.

"So let me spell it out for you. Play the game. It's a great game. Savour the opportunity you have to play with the best in the world. Then smile nice for the cameras and get the hell away from the rink. Not just physically, but in your head too. Then go home to your family. If you go home and choose to really *be* with them, then they'll give you all the love you could ask for. And it will be for *you*. Not for your status. Not for your hockey card. For you."

Kevin smiled, impressed by the wisdom of his old coach. "So how do you know all this stuff?"

Gord shrugged, embarrassed by the credit, "well . . . you screw up enough times, you eventually figure this stuff out," he responded quickly out of habit. Then he paused and looked up thoughtfully. "Honestly, Kevin . . . when a man is facing death, the bottom lines reveal themselves much more easily. You're able to see what's truly important. What's truly beautiful about life. It separates easily from all the bullshit that used to distract you from it. Kind of an ironic gift for someone whose life is about to end."

Kevin's expression turned to one of concern. "Ah, come on, Cormie. You're not gonna die. You'll get through this," he insisted.

"Well, we'll see. The missus has been through so much already. And this thing seems to have me by the throat." Gord saw Kevin fighting back tears, and chose to rescue him one more time, "Ah, maybe you're right, kid. Maybe I can win this period. This shift feels like a good one."

11

"How's your little brother doing?" Gord asked, moving the conversation along.

"Um . . . I'm not sure. I still haven't talked to him." Kevin looked embarrassed with his answer. Several times, Cormie had suggested that he call him. Each time, Kevin assured him that he would.

"Still haven't, eh?" Gord confirmed, not trying very hard to hide his disappointment. "You know, Kev, one thing I'm learning through all this is the importance of tying up loose ends."

Kevin looked up at him, waiting for elaboration.

"I've spent a lot of time on the phone in the last few months, tracking down people that I said I'd call and forgot to, talking to family, checking in on former players to see how they're doing now. And they all seemed very appreciative to hear from me, and very forgiving that I'd lost touch with them in the first place."

"He said some really shitty things the last time we spoke, Cormie," Kevin said, defending himself uncertainly.

"I know Kevin, we've been through this. But were some of them true?" Gord knew this was a gamble, but felt it was time for it.

Kevin paused, feeling completely transparent to Cormie. It's true that his brother's attack on him had been riddled with comments he wanted desperately to dismiss, but on some level, he had a hard time pretending there was no truth to them. "I don't know. I'm starting to see a lot of things differently right now. I think I need time to let my head settle."

Gord nodded, content with the response. He just wanted Kevin to think about his brother, to consider reconnecting with him somehow. He was sitting on the bed, leaning against the wall. His eyes looked heavy.

"You want to sleep for a little while, Cormie?"

"Maybe for a little while. You want to go get a coffee with the girls?" Gord asked, searching for a way to keep Kevin around for more visiting.

"I'll just stay here, Cormie. Maybe I'll mute the T.V. and watch a little."

"Thanks Kev. It's great to see you."

"You too, Cormie. Try to get a little rest." Kevin covered Gord's shoulders with the covers as he slid under. He watched him fall asleep instantly, hoping their visit wasn't too tiring for Cormie when his body needed the rest. As he sat next to the bed, Kevin's mind wandered to thoughts of his younger brother, Brad.

As a kid, Brad had idolized Kevin. With three years between them, Brad took an interest in hockey about the same time people started noticing Kevin's potential as a player. From that point on, Brad had a two-in-one brother/hero. He hung around him whenever he could. Kevin was flattered at times, annoyed at others. As a teen, it's not very cool to have your younger brother tagging along all the time.

Brad watched Kevin's every move on the ice and tried to mimic him in his own games. He anxiously awaited his graduation to peewee hockey, when body contact is introduced. He couldn't wait to take the body like his big brother, Kev. But Brad had his mother's stature. He was of average height, willowy in frame. So Brad was feisty, but not as daunting a physical threat as Kevin.

But like Kevin's, Brad's skills grew steadily with the countless hours that they spent at the outdoor rink close to their house. And the hockey in Medicine Hat was just competitive enough to push them each year. The hockey community in their town touted 'Big Wilk' and 'Little Wilk' as sure NHLers.

But when it became clearer that Brad would not have Kevin's frame, Brad stopped taking pro hockey for granted. He spent more and more time on his studies, applying the same determination that allowed him to excel on the ice to his schooling, where he was equally impressive.

Interestingly, with his academics to fall back on, Brad's playing ability soared, breaking the Medicine Hat Bantam single season scoring record that his brother had set three years earlier. Kevin wondered how much better Brad could have been if he focused more exclusively on hockey. Brad saw it differently.

For a long time, Brad had felt that he *had to* perform on the ice, that failing to live up to his brother would be devastating. So he had been motivated by fear. But he discovered that fear can be a powerful motivator in the short term, but lousy in the long run. The expectations of the community and his father became his own. And his love of the game waned with each new expectation he had for himself. But having discovered other talents of his own, Brad had let go of the pressure that he had previously accepted.

The ice became a playground again. He was more creative, less apprehensive, and a very easy guy to play with. It mattered to him that everyone else have fun too. He lightened locker rooms that were heavy with expectations. He restored passion to hearts where big league hopes dwindled. And for a time, the game was his sanctuary from the reality that his father was gone.

But eventually, Brad's curse was his ability. Expectations grew exponentially when he became the hometown prodigy, making the Medicine Hat Tiger squad as a 15 year-old. Brad was again seduced by the attention that success provided, buying into the importance of his success to the people around him. Their mother felt this shift back to the pressures of the game was tied to Brad's failed attempts to reconnect with his father.

His major junior experience was a frustrating one. He didn't put up the numbers that had been projected, although he was still good enough by his third year to play on the first line, still only seventeen. The local sports writers continued to make comparisons between 'Big and Little Wilk', constantly reminding him of his shortcomings, while Kevin enjoyed a promising rookie season in the NHL. The game again lost its luster, and Brad contemplated a move to university hockey, where he could pursue his studies seriously.

Along the way, Kevin had been supportive. He'd been Brad's number one fan, even when they played against each other. He encouraged Brad to 'keep plugging' amidst the frustration. "You've got the heart of a lion, Brad. You'll get there. You've just got to believe." And Brad continued to battle as best he could, not wanting to let his brother down. Kevin had believed in him all along. He felt he owed his brother something, although he wasn't sure what.

Then came the event that would disillusion Brad permanently about the nature of elite hockey, and ultimately, would drive a wedge between him and his brother. The general manager of the Medicine Hat Tigers, Murray Sobel, had been one of Brad's supporters, turning down trade offers from other teams whose managers felt Brad's abilities would be better suited to their systems. Brad had asked Sobel in confidence to keep him in Medicine Hat, so that he could continue living with his mother, who would otherwise be alone with the departure of her husband and older son. It struck Sobel as an uncommonly altruistic request from a player and he agreed.

But after Christmas, in his third year, Brad shared with Sobel his decision to accept a scholarship at the University of Saskatchewan, where he would pursue a degree in biology, an area that fascinated him. Sobel pleaded with him to reconsider, citing statistics on how few Canadian university players go on to play professionally. Brad assured him that his decision was made, and Sobel, in turn, thanked him for being so forthcoming and assured him that he would finish his major junior career in a Tigers' uniform.

Kevin was equally unimpressed with the decision, asking repeatedly why he would "piss away a shot at a pro career". None of Brad's answers satisfied him, and eventually, he called less often, not wanting to have the same argument. Then at the trade deadline, Brad was delivered a blow.

Sobel had traded him to the Spokane Chiefs. In his final semester, he was pulled out of the only high school he'd ever been to. He had already started studying for his diploma exams, which would be critical, not only to graduate, but also for the academic scholarships for which he was eligible. The American system was completely different, incompatible with the courses he was taking in Medicine Hat.

After a few days of scrambling, he had arranged to continue his Canadian courses through correspondence with his teachers, then would return to write the exams in Medicine Hat that June. He felt indebted to his instructors, but was also nervous about how well he could do from a distance. Above all he felt betrayed by Sobel, and victimized by the 'hockey business'.

Things went from bad to worse for Brad, when he went to Spokane. He found out that the Spokane general manager, Ron Sumner, had not been told about his intentions at season's end. Sumner had given up Spokane's top defenseman on a hunch that Wilkins would have a breakthrough season as an 18 year-old. Sobel denied having any knowledge of Brad's intentions.

After the Spokane media caught wind of the situation and aired the fiasco, the Spokane fans quickly turned on Brad, booing him whenever he touched the puck, jeering him when he was on the bench. With only one assist in four games as a Chief, Brad packed his belongings and, telling no one, not even his billets, he boarded a bus for Calgary, then another back to Medicine Hat.

As Kevin flipped through the muted channels on Cormie's hospital room television, he replayed in his head the argument that he and Brad had had when Brad returned to Medicine Hat from Spokane four years earlier.

"Hello, Brad?" Kevin asked sharply.

"Hey, Kev. I thought you might call."

"Damn right, someone's got to talk some sense into you. Mom obviously couldn't," Kevin barked, his volume rising.

"Leave Mom out of this, Kev. She hasn't tried to talk me out of it because she knows I was right." Brad responded, not intimidated by his brother's tone. "Because you're *right*?" Kevin asked incredulously. "Jesus Christ, Brad! This is suicide for your playing career! No one's gonna want anything to do with you if . . ."

Brad cut in, "I'm done, Kevin! I'm finished! I don't want to play pro hockey badly enough to get yanked around and treated like this! That's it!"

Kevin paused, then lowered his tone, "You chickenshit."

"What?" Brad asked, both confused and annoyed.

"You're so afraid that you won't live up to me that you won't even give it a shot," Kevin announced, thinking he'd hit the target.

"Oh my God, Kev! You don't get it. You're so obsessed with the game that you can't see anything outside of it. I don't want that life! I have other things that I want to do with my life. There *are* more important things than hockey." Brad knew this would strike a nerve.

"So that's it? You got kicked in the gut, and now you're just gonna crumble? It's a tough business, Brad. It's not for the weak. But I thought you had the balls to make it." Kevin voice rang with disappointment.

"You arrogant prick! You may be nothing without hockey, Kev, but I'm not. When I pack it in, life will begin. When you're done; your life is over. You're nothing."

Kevin remembered the fight like it was yesterday. *How could he have given up the dream so easily? The dream we shared growing up. Worse yet, how could he turn on me like that?* Kevin wondered after the mental audio finished playing. Then for the first time, Kevin wondered if he had been wrong.

12

"You actually watching this, Wilk?" Gord asked.

A cooking program was on the T.V. Kevin had long since stopped paying attention to it, although he had instinctively continued to flick up and down the channels.

"No, I was just thinking," Kevin responded, drifting back into the present.

"About Brad?" Gord asked, hopefully.

Kevin exhaled sharply through his nose, almost a silent laugh. "How do you do that?"

"That was just a guess actually. It's the last thing we were talking about before my nap. How long was I sleeping?"

Kevin glanced down at his watch, surprised at how much time had gone by. "Wow, almost an hour."

Gord went back to his point, as if they hadn't stopped talking, "So, was some of what Brad said to you true?"

"Maybe. The stinger was when he said I was nobody without hockey."

"Ah yes," Gord said, remembering what Kevin had told him. "So are you?"

"Well, I don't think so, but you might get an argument from Erin on that one." Kevin replied, unsure what to believe.

"Kev, do you remember what you told me when you came over to tell me you were planning to propose to Erin?" Gord looked smug, like he'd just solved a riddle.

"Not really. It was a long time ago. I probably told you lots of things. I was pretty excited." Kevin recalled the mood, not the words.

"Well, you told me something that made Lorna and I confident that Erin was the right girl for you. Although Lorna thought she was a great catch the first time she met her," Gord said, getting sidetracked.

Kevin squinted, searching his memory.

"You said that Erin made you feel like more than a hockey player," Gord finally said, letting him in on the riddle.

Kevin said nothing, now glued to Gord and listening intently.

"Look, Kev, the two people who were closest to you both had basically the same criticism of you, that you had become one-dimensional, depending on hockey for who you are. The more you bought into the superstar status, the more distracted you became from your relationships with each of them. You and Rick Olsen still close?" Kevin pressed his face into his hands, feeling like his life had been spilled all over the hospital floor, "No, not really."

"You see, there's another guy that could help you stay connected to the right things. Olse is a great kid," Gord mused, getting sidetracked again. Kevin was too rattled to respond.

"So who do you hang out with on the road? I know it's not Koshenko," he said jokingly. "Tell me it's not that Morrison character." Gord laughed as he asked.

Kevin dropped his head, closed his eyes, and started to chuckle. No one could read him like Cormie, not even Erin. But there was something comfortable about feeling so completely understood. Cormie wouldn't like him any less, knowing all that he knew. If anything, he'd like him a little more. That was Cormie. If he decided he liked you, there was almost nothing you could do to change it.

By this time, both men were laughing. Amazingly, Gord's lungs were not irritated by his belly laugh. As both Kevin and Gord wiped a tear from laughing so hard, the women returned from the cafeteria.

"Looks like you two are having a grand old time," Lorna said, thrilled to see her husband in such good spirits.

Erin smiled at Kevin, wondering what she had missed. "Um, Lorna and I were going to pick up some hamburgers from across the street. There's a Wendy's over there. Does that interest you guys?"

"A couple Big Classics with cheese would be awesome," Kevin replied.

"Sure, one of those sounds great. Here, I'll give you guys some money," Gord said reaching for his jacket.

"We've got this one, Cormie," Erin answered quickly, pushing Gord's jacket out of his reach.

"Thanks, you guys," Kevin offered, realizing how hungry he was.

"See you shortly, boys," Lorna said, looking more relaxed than when they first arrived. "You two try to stay out of trouble," she added, smiling.

Kevin looked over at Gord and shrugged, "No psych ward panty raid, I guess . . . sorry buddy," he said playfully.

Everyone laughed, welcoming the comic relief. Erin's giggles were perhaps the loudest, excited to see Kevin in such a spontaneous state.

As the two women disappeared around the corner, Gord turned to Kevin, his face becoming somber. "You have to tell her, Kev."

Kevin's head turned very slowly, his eyes pleading for understanding about what he was about to say, "I can't, Cormie. It would kill her. I can't hurt her like that."

"Kevin," Gord's tone deepened.

"No, Cormie, listen. I fucked up . . . big time, and what I've been doing is horrible, but telling her would only hurt her. And what about Tory?" Kevin read Gord's face, realizing his last comment was a mistake.

"Don't you bring her into this, Kevin, especially not as an excuse not to be truthful." For the first time since their arrival, Gord was angry. "What if it had been her, Kev?"

Kevin pressed his hands together in front of his mouth, trying to wish the conversation to an end. Then he finally spoke, his voice quiet and resigned, "I know. I'd want to know."

Gord sat back and nodded, relieved that his point had been acknowledged. "But say I do tell her. Then what? She'll leave me and take Tory with her. She's forgiven me for things in the past, but nothing like this. This is too much." Kevin leaned forward, trying desperately to convince his friend. "I'm finally seeing things clearly. Things can be so much better again . . . but not if I tell her. We'd have no chance."

"Alright Kev, forget about her for a moment. How has not telling her affected *you*?"

Kevin said nothing, just stared straight ahead. He felt trapped because he knew where the conversation was going. He knew Cormie was right, without even hearing what he was about to say. Gord leaned forward, placing his hand on Kevin's shoulder. "Kevin, I love you like a son. And I wouldn't press you on this unless I thought it was in your best interests. Some guys can screw around on their girlfriends and wives and not give it a second thought. You're not one of those guys. As a player, you carried guilt around like a suitcase, because you never wanted to let me or the team down. You couldn't clear your head until we sat down and talked about it. As a husband, I'm sure that you're the same way. I know how much you love Erin. You used to talk about her so much, you drove the other guys nuts. I know this must be eating away at you inside, like the cancer in my lungs."

Kevin still stared straight ahead, sitting motionless in the chair next to the bed. "Stop me if I'm wrong, Kev, but I have a pretty good guess at how the past year has gone for you. You probably got a little full of yourself and that got to Erin. She closed up, although only for a while. That made you mad. You got quiet. You retaliated with your own silence, doubling your affection to Tory to emphasize your point. Then you were both mad, mad enough to mess around with someone else. Then the quiet became a necessity, because you then had to maintain two different worlds: the one in which you were faithful, . . . and reality. You were afraid to slip up, so you shut up. And turned the gap between you into an abyss".

Kevin's eyes were now glassy, and a tear appeared under his eye, then slowly made its way down his cheek. He finally turned to Gord, his face bewildered by his coach's apparent clairvoyance. "Did Olse call you? Did he tell you all this?"

"No Kev, I've just seen it before. A marriage can't be held together by a lie. How long before you put your feelings on her, and become jealous at the drop of a hat? If it was meant to be, you guys will get through it. I'm not saying it won't be ugly at first, but it's the right thing, Kev. You know it is. If you're seeing things clearly now, then keep it that way. Pretending it didn't happen will cloud your vision. And every time you share a nice moment with your wife, it'll be tainted; you'll feel like you're getting away with something you shouldn't."

Kevin took a deep breath and sank down into his chair. "Alright, I'll tell her. But I need time to prepare myself for it."

"Sure, kid. Like game day," Gord added, giving Kevin license to choose his own timing.

"Man, maybe I should just have gone to a counselor," Kevin said, summoning the strength to smile.

"Oh, was this visit *instead of* a counsellor? Gord asked, fairly sure he got the joke.

"Yeah, I said you're the closest thing I've had to that, and Jamie Harris talked Bouche into it."

"Jamie Harris. He seemed like a pretty good guy the few times we've met," Gord said, lightening the conversation.

"Yeah, Bones is great. I'm not sure why we call him that," Kevin added, still puzzled by the nickname.

"So where do I send the bill?" Gord asked, making a futile attempt at a straight face.

Kevin smiled, acknowledging the joke, but still lost in the seriousness of their discussion. For a moment, he sat quietly, reflecting on all that had been said. Gord knew not to interrupt his thoughts. As his coach, Gord had recognized Kevin's tendency to defend himself when under criticism, then to quietly absorb the message in its entirety and act on it. Few of his players ever developed the maturity to take this second step. But the gravity of this discussion was a true test of Kevin's ability to listen . . . and to trust. Gord watched Kevin's face intently, searching for a sign that he had come to some sort of peace. For a moment, he saw what he interpreted as a look of acceptance. Not contentment, for his expression still was heavy with the responsibilities that he had to his family. But it looked like he had stopped fighting what he knew deep down, and had accepted his executive role in resetting his course.

As Gord sank back onto the bed, hopeful that their discussion would have a lasting impact, Kevin's expression shifted, as if something was just dawning on him. Kevin seemed to 'come to', as he looked around at his surroundings. Finally, as he turned to Gord, he took a deep breath, and asked the question that his fear had inhibited to that point.

"So . . . just how bad is this thing?"

Gord felt the heaviness of his own condition rise to his consciousness. He had lost himself temporarily in the task of helping his young friend. Gord again contemplated his option of protecting Kevin from the truth, then quickly abandoned it. Kevin had shared the ugliness of his own life, opening himself completely, lowering his defenses. Gord recognized that he now had only one obligation to his friend, to be truthful. To share of himself as Kevin had.

"The surgeon was pretty optimistic after the first of the cancer was taken out. He said it came out neatly and appeared to be isolated to a few spots. Then the chemo absolutely kicked the crap out of me. But as horrible as I felt, I was confident that we'd seen the last of it. But this time it's a lot worse. The docs have been thrown by how quickly this has come back," Gord looked into Kevin's eyes, sparing him nothing, "and it's come back with a vengeance, Kev."

He paused, wishing there wasn't more bad news to the story. Kevin said nothing. Gord's jaw tightened, fighting off his desperate need to cry. "They said that, given the way this thing has come back, there's an awfully good chance it could turn up somewhere else, even if the surgery goes well." Stumbling over the last few words, Gord began to sob. His arms curled into his body, like those of a fetus. Kevin stood up, now crying himself, searching in vain for a way to take Cormie's hurt away. He reached around Gord with both arms, and pulled him in, burying his own face in his coach's shoulder. Gord was limp in Kevin's arms, now completely broken down.

"I'm not ready to die, Kev. But I don't think I can beat this." Both men wept for several minutes. Kevin never loosened his embrace.

Lorna and Erin appeared around the corner, still laughing from their own conversation. The condition of the two men registered quickly for Lorna. She walked calmly over to them and reached around them, kissing Gord on the cheek, and Kevin on the head.

Erin was at once confused and distressed. She walked over and reached around Kevin's waist, resting her head on his back. The four were silent for over a minute. All pretenses were gone. All defenses down. Only the very core of their humanity remained.

13

The Olsens' house.

Rick and Kate Olsen sat at the kitchen table drinking tea, watching the girls play in the living room. The oldest girl, Meaghan, was up in her room on the phone, a common occurrence in her grade-six year. Seven year-old Kayla assumed a leadership role in organizing the doll tea party. Bethany and Tory played along, content to follow her lead.

Kate smiled contently while she waited for her tea to cool. Rick looked far away, apparently in a trance. His face showed no obvious signs of emotion or mood.

"Tired, Hun?" Kate inquired.

"A little," he answered, blinking out of his distant state. Kate knew now that his mind was busy with something.

"What's on your mind?" Kate probed, turning in her seat to give Rick her full attention.

"I was just thinking about Kev actually."

Kate nodded, her expression turning serious. "Does he seem different to you lately?" she asked, trying to link her conversation with Erin to Rick's thoughts.

Rick looked back at Kate, deciding whether to finally disclose what he knew. He paused, took a deep breath and let it out slowly. Kate knew this couldn't be good news.

"What is it, Rick?"

Rick turned his eyes away from Kate, glancing toward the living room to make sure the girls were out of earshot. "Kev's been unfaithful. He's been sleeping around on the road."

Kate sat back in her chair, not particularly surprised at the news. She had suspected that this might be the case. Her face took on a whole new uneasiness as she searched Rick's face for hints of his thoughts. The silence became too uncomfortable, so she filled it. "How long?"

"Most of this season for sure. I don't know how long before that," he replied, still resistant to look at her.

"Did he tell you?" Kate asked, struggling to get the details.

"No. But enough guys know, and they joke in the room about those kinds of things. You know . . . it's not that unusual. Anyway . . . Erin's such a good kid. I just don't get why he'd do that."

Kate stood up and walked to the counter, facing the cupboard, away from Rick. He knew immediately what she was thinking. He got up and walked quickly over to her. He wrapped his arms around her from behind, placing his head on her shoulder. "That was different, Kate. And we've put that behind us. It was a long time ago."

Kate pulled Rick's hands tighter to her chest and tried to smile. "Come on," Rick said, as he let go and took Kate by the hand. He led her into the living room, where the girls were playing.

"Can Mommy and I play, you guys?" Rick asked, looking at Kayla who seemed to be in charge.

"Sure," Kayla said, still focused on setting up the dolls the way she wanted them. She handed a doll to Kate, "You can play with Hannah," she said, with a motherly tone. "And you can play with Bruno," she added, handing Rick a stuffed teddy bear.

Rick and Kate knelt down and joined in, careful not to disrupt the flow of the play already in progress. Kate looked over at Rick, mouthing the words 'I love you', her eyes looking a little glassy. He leaned over and kissed her on the cheek. Kayla and Bethany continued to play, accustomed to their parents' open affection towards each other. Tory stopped to watch them, smiling curiously. Rick looked down at her, kneeling beside them. He touched her on the nose playfully, smiling back at her. She giggled, then returned to playing, quickly re-engaging in the tea party.

14

Erin walked out of the hotel bathroom in her robe, still drying her hair. They had decided to call it a day and let Gord get some rest. Erin stopped and looked at Kevin, who was sitting motionless on the bed, still in his towel, staring blankly at the floor. He felt her looking at him but did not look up. His eyes closed and his lids gently squeezed a tear from the outer corner of both eyes. *Why Cormie? Why does this have to happen to him? Of all people.* Kevin asked in his mind, receiving no answers.

Erin sat down next to him on the bed, her brow wrinkled with concern. She wanted him to know how much she loved him, and that he was not, and would never be alone with his feelings. But she knew that he was past words, that the message would have to come in a different form if it was to have a chance at being received.

Erin stood and faced her husband, placing her hands on his shoulders. Leaning over, she wiped his tears away softly with her thumbs and climbed delicately onto his lap. She kissed him softly on each cheek, then on each eyelid. Absorbed by Kevin's emotions, she felt tears of her own making their way down her cheeks. Reaching around him with both arms, she pulled herself close to him. Pressing her cheek against his, their tears mixed on each other's face. Erin continued to kiss Kevin's face, alternating side to side, tasting the salt of their tears.

Guiding his chin with her hand, she lightly pressed her lips against his. Kevin kissed back, his eyes still closed, finally responding to her. As they kissed, Erin felt him stirring involuntarily beneath his towel. She was momentarily ashamed that she had aroused him in his moment of weakness, then surrendered to the wave of intimacy that embraced them. Without breaking their kiss, she reached down and slid the towel away.

She slowly aligned herself with him, then slid down, pressing him inside of her. They continued to kiss, with Erin moving her hips slowly and rhythmically in circles. She felt Kevin's tears rolling down her stomach, then felt his hands around her hips as he moved gently to her rhythm. As their movement intensified, Erin leaned back slightly, holding Kevin's shoulders. She dropped her head back, whimpering slightly, sensation rippling through her, then felt Kevin contract inside of her.

He pulled her close, his eyes still closed, and rested his face against her neck. His breathing slowed, and he lifted his head, finally opening his eyes. Kevin looked deep into Erin's eyes, kissed her forehead and spoke, "I'm so lucky to have you." Erin smiled, wiping away the remnants of her own tears. "Well, get used to it, Wilk. Because you're always gonna have me" she replied, sighing pleasantly, like she was smiling out loud.

Minutes later, Kevin lay watching Erin sleep, unable to fall asleep himself. His thoughts had returned to Cormie, less about the cancer than the relationship that they shared. He wished that he had told Cormie how he truly felt about him before they'd left for the evening. But he felt the opportunity had disappeared when Gord seemed to tire so rapidly.

Lorna was unable to have children. Gord had once confided that the one thing he felt was missing from his life was children. Kevin affirmed for his coach that he would have been a great father. What Kevin hadn't brought himself to say was that he considered Gord to be like a father to him. In truth, Cormie's manner with people was what Kevin aspired to as Tory's father. He wanted her to feel how he felt around Cormie: accepted, challenged, . . . loved. He had always struggled to get out his most profound sentiments, not wanting to sound sappy or weak. But he knew that telling Cormie what he really felt put him at risk for neither. He rolled over, content with his decision. *Tomorrow. Tomorrow I'll tell him everything.*

15

When morning came, Kevin seemed decidedly upbeat. He couldn't wait to get to the hospital to see Cormie. It was the day before his surgery, and Kevin was determined to help him prepare. Erin was relieved to see Kevin in such a positive state, thinking that Kevin's energy would no doubt rub off on Gord, at this critical time in his struggle.

At breakfast, Kevin shared with Erin what he planned to say to Cormie. He felt ashamed that it had taken these circumstances to rouse it in him, but figured, "better late than never". Erin beamed with pride as he spoke, simultaneously hopeful for Gord, and thrilled that fatherhood was so important to Kevin.

Outside the doors of the hospital, Kevin stopped to make a quick call.

"Hi, you've reached Jamie Harris, assistant coach of the Vancouver Canucks. I'm either on the phone or away from my desk . . .". Kevin knew he'd get Bones' machine with the time difference. He didn't want to have to defend his decision to stay overnight and miss practice. He wanted to simply leave a message and deal with the consequences later.

"Hi Bones, Wilk here. Meeting with Gord McCormack has been really helpful. I'll be in Calgary for another day or so. Sorry about missing practice, but I think this is the best thing for me right now. I'll talk to you when I get back." He turned off his phone and he and Erin walked into the hospital.

When they walked into Gord's room, no one was there. The bed had been made and none of Cormie's belongings remained. Kevin cut his panic off quickly, conjuring an explanation, "He must have changed rooms. Probably a different room because of his surgery tomorrow." Erin said nothing, fearing the worst.

"Well, let's go track him down," Kevin said, taking Erin's hand. Despite keeping a cool tone, Kevin's worry was apparent to Erin. His grip on her hand was vice-like, and she almost had to jog to keep up with him on the way out of the room. As they approached the nursing station, a young nurse stood up, as if she was expecting them.

"Mr. and Mrs. Wilkins?" she inquired. They nodded, waiting nervously to find out why she knew who they were. Kevin hoped she was just a hockey fan.

"I'm afraid I have some bad news," she said, still young enough in her career to feel guilty in delivering such a message, "Mr. McCormack passed away last night."

Erin covered her mouth with both hands, already starting to cry. It was too sudden for Kevin to get his head around it.

"What? No, he can't . . . we were just here with him last night. He was fine."

"I'm sorry Mr. Wilkins."

"They just moved him somewhere else. He has surgery tomorrow." Kevin tried to will his alternative explanation onto the reality. Erin tried to interrupt, "Kev. Kev, honey?" He didn't hear her.

The nurse shook her head, let him finish, then explained, "he had what's called a pulmonary embolism. It's a blood clot in the lungs. It happened very quickly, before anything could be done."

Kevin had already turned away from the nurse. He pressed his hands into his forehead and stepped away, overwhelmed.

"Where's Mrs. McCormack?" Erin asked, trying to hold herself together long enough to get some answers.

"She was with him earlier. She may be in the chapel now," the nurse responded, tilting her head sympathetically.

Kevin turned to the nurse, now appearing angry, "he was staying here so that nothing like this would happen. He was supposed to be safe here."

"Mr. Wilkins, we did everything we could to help him. It just happened too quickly. I'm very sorry." Her tone was firm but compassionate. Kevin leaned over onto the counter, folding his arms and hiding his face. His anger had suddenly been washed away by a wave of grief. Erin put her hands on his shoulders for support. She felt him start to tremble, no longer able to hold back the tears.

He stood up and pulled Erin in, his face pressed against the side of her head. His head was swimming with thoughts. *Why Cormie? Why couldn't we have one more day? How could I cheat him of the things that I never said? Did he know how I felt?* He squeezed Erin tighter as he gave in to his emotions. He had lost his dearest friend, his surrogate father, his hero.

For this moment, he stopped fighting his feelings. He cried for several minutes, oblivious to the other people in the corridor. He was not ashamed. He cried because he'd lost someone dear to him, someone that mattered to him. He cried to honour his friend.

Finally, he took a deep breath and taking a tissue from the counter, wiped his eyes and his nose. Sensing he was finished for now, Erin leaned in and whispered, "Let's go find Lorna."

16

Kevin and Erin peeked into the small hospital chapel. Lorna sat alone in the front pew. As they walked quietly toward her, they could tell that she had been crying. Her eyes looked heavy and sore. Faint marks from her eye make-up remained, mostly washed and rubbed away. She held a handful of tissue tight in her fist. Her other hand rubbed her knee, forward and back, thoughtlessly, like an autistic child rocks. Her expression looked numb, like she was either in shock or exhausted from her initial bout with grief. She stared at the floor, seldom blinking.

Erin leaned over, placing both hands on Lorna's shoulders. Lorna stiffened at the touch, then relaxed and closed her eyes. Erin rested her cheek against Lorna's and spoke very softly, almost whispering, "I'm so sorry." Lorna nodded, reaching for Erin's hand on her shoulder, her eyes still closed. A single tear made it's way down the moistened cheek of Gord's widow, stopping when it reached Erin's face. Erin reached around with both arms from where she stood behind, squeezing gently.

Kevin stood watching. He looked at Lorna as if for the first time. Despite the age that the crying had added, she looked young to him, much younger than his mother, although they were about the same age. He could not remember how old she was, only that she seemed far too young to be in this position, mourning the loss of her husband. Kevin walked around her and sat down next to her. He leaned forward, folding his hands, and stared straight ahead. The three were motionless for several minutes.

Finally, Kevin sat back against the pew and turned his head towards Lorna, not quite looking at her. He cleared his throat then swallowed, preparing himself to speak.

"I never told him that he was like a father to me." His eyes narrowed slightly, angered by his own words.

"He knew, dear. With all his heart, he knew." Lorna had somehow summoned the strength to open her eyes and look directly at Kevin. "And he loved you like you were his own, Kevin."

Kevin's eyes welled up and his chest heaved, his breath quickened by the emotion that Lorna's words conjured. He tilted towards her, starting to sob again. Lorna pulled his head in under her chin. She cried silently now. Her tears rolled like a stream down her face but her body was still, her maternal instincts seeking to calm her surrogate child.

Erin sat awkwardly behind them, pained by her husband's grief. She wanted to take his hurt away. Then she finally sat back in her seat, resigned to the fact that she could not. In fact, maybe she should not, for this was something that he needed to feel.

When Kevin finished crying, Lorna sat him up and turned herself to face him squarely. "Could you say a few words at the service?" she asked. Kevin nodded.

Erin marveled at Lorna's strength, hoping that she might one day acquire her resilience. What Erin didn't know was that Lorna had privately commenced her grieving process long before this day had come, careful not to let Gord see anything other than hope and courage. This day she was finally not alone with her tears, strangely soothed by the presence of Kevin and the honesty in his grief.

17

Vancouver. Canucks practice.

Rick Olsen led the way through a tough skate, still setting the standard for on-ice fitness at thirty-three. The team went through a long series of 'flow' drills, resetting their aerobic levels after the day off. All of the players appeared to be labouring, except for Vlad Koshenko, not because of exceptional fitness, but rather due to a naturally superior skating stride that had been honed on a larger ice surface overseas. Billy Morrison kept pace with Rick and Vlad, more out of determination than fitness or skill.

The hard skate was not punishment for the Dallas loss, but rather a recommendation of the training staff, attempting to sustain the team's fitness going into the play-offs. But most of the players attributed hard conditioning to angry coaches, despite attempts to educate them otherwise. Nothing had been said about Kevin's absence, although Rick knew it was only a matter of time.

A little over an hour earlier, Kate had called Rick on his cell phone to tell him that Erin had called. While he was walking into the rink, Rick had wondered if Gord McCormack's failing health had been on Kevin's mind in Dallas when he blew up. The distance that had grown between Kevin and Rick dissolved in Rick's mind as his big-brotherly instincts took over. Whether or not McCormack's health was a factor in Kevin's behaviour, Rick knew that Kevin was going to need a friend. Kevin had spoken fondly of 'Cormie' in conversations with Rick. He had also spoken of him often, which Rick took as a sign that the coach held a position of great significance in Kevin's eyes.

But when Rick stepped on the ice for practice, he entertained no thoughts that did not pertain to hockey and preparation for Edmonton the next night. A win against Edmonton would move them into a tie with the Oilers for seventh place, with a final regular season game at hand, one that they expected to win against a struggling Anaheim squad.

The players leaned against the boards, trying to catch their breath enough to drink without sucking water down their wind pipes. Rick was commenting to Kyle Kopp about the speedy Edmonton forwards when he heard Conrad Soles speaking behind him.

"Nice of Wilk to show up. We've got him to thank for this and he's not even fuckin' here."

"You can use the work, Conrad. Don't worry about Wilk," Rick replied.

"Well, where the hell is he? Taking a little holiday during his suspension?" Soles demanded, upset by Rick's intervention.

"I said, don't worry about him, Conrad. He wouldn't miss without a good reason. Did you do all the summer workouts?" Rick asked, deflecting the focus onto Soles. Soles didn't respond. Rick nodded, sure of the answer, then added, "Right. You just take care of getting yourself ready."

All of the surrounding players were quiet, surprised at the tension in Rick's tone. There was a long silence then Rick put down his water bottle and put is glove back on, pushing away from the boards, and gliding towards center, as if to communicate to the whole group that the break had been long enough. Conrad Soles muttered under his breath to the goalie, Mark Dorsey, "Great, now he's even got Olse kissin' his ass."

Rick spun around quickly, facing Soles. "One more word and we fuckin' go, Conrad! Right now!" Rick's voice took on a tone laced with aggression. Soles stood facing Rick, looking him in the eyes. He was significantly bigger than Rick, and had dropped the gloves several times this season, compared to once by Rick. But Olsen had a pitbull reputation from earlier in his career, one that Soles didn't care to resurrect. Rick's piercing stare was amply convincing. Conrad knew he would not win this fight, nor was he being paid for it. He pursed his lips, and looked away, shaking his head in subtle protest, then skated towards center ice for the next drill.

After practice, Rick headed straight into Marcel Boucher's office, closing the door behind him. The coaching staff needed to know why Kevin was missing. They would also want to know why a fight had nearly started in practice, two games away from the play-offs. Rick decided to kill both birds with one stone. Boucher stopped unlacing his skates and sat back in his chair, his eyebrows raised and mouth closed, awaiting an explanation. Rick sat sideways on the desk and began, "I know why Wilk's not here."

18

Calgary International Airport. 6:15 that same day.

With the quick arrival of some of Lorna's friends and relatives, she insisted that Kevin and Erin could go back to Vancouver. The memorial service would not be for a few days, and Lorna knew that Kevin already had to answer for a missed practice. Erin offered to stay for support, but Lorna assured her that she had lots of support on the way and that Tory would be missing her mother by now.

Kevin and Erin sat quietly, holding hands, waiting for their flight to board. Both were emotionally exhausted and partly relieved that they were heading home. Kevin was already a little nervous about speaking at the memorial. He was a pretty good speaker, especially for a hockey player, but he felt that Cormie deserved a very special eulogy, perhaps more special than what he could prepare.

Erin's thoughts were of Tory. She'd been missing her ever since Lorna mentioned her earlier that day. Her concerns about her marriage had dissolved over the course of those couple of days. Despite the solemn occasion that brought them to Calgary, she felt that both she and Kevin were somehow better connected to themselves and to each other through the experience. She'd seen more of the Kevin that she fell in love with in those two days than she had all year, and was hopeful that he was back to stay. He seemed both open and *real* to her again.

As the plane ascended, Kevin watched the ground shrink below. As he assembled anecdotes and events in his mind that could colour his tribute to Cormie, he felt progressively ashamed that he was not making the kind of contribution to the lives of others that Cormie had. What had he admired in Cormie? His love for living. His acceptance of others. His undying energy to teach and encourage. His devotion to the people that he cared about.

The vague uneasiness that Kevin had felt a week earlier had crystallized. He had traded in the attributes that he liked most in himself for a turn in the spotlight. He accepted the demigod status of 'professional athlete' in exchange for the real him. He had been falsely humble in front of the media, never truly believing his own words. He had seen his stardom as something to which he was entitled, forgetting to share the credit with the people who had helped to get him there, forgetting that many others who worked just as hard had fallen short of their dreams.

The loss of Cormie had woken him from the illusion that he'd been living in, where hockey was what life was all about, instead of people. Where winning was most important, not playing. He made a living *playing* the *game* of hockey. When was the last time he had truly played? When was the last time he saw it as a game?

He pondered what part hockey had played in Cormie's life. True, Cormie loved the game, but was hockey the be-all end-all of his existence? Of course not. Cormie's passion was for people, and for the spontaneous spirit of those engaged in play. Hockey had simply been a vehicle to experience those things.

Although he felt ashamed over lost time, Kevin now felt responsible for refocusing his own life. He began assembling the priorities that would give real meaning to his life, and add value to the people around him. While he drafted Cormie's eulogy in his head, he highlighted the ways in which *he* wanted to be remembered. In a sense, he began writing the eulogy that he wanted people to hear after his own death.

Kevin looked down at Erin who had fallen asleep on his shoulder. Despite the closeness that he had reacquired with her, he still felt that one secret stood in the way of the connection that they had once shared. Cormie had insisted that Kevin confess that he'd been unfaithful. But he felt trapped. Not telling her would always be a form of distance between them. But he felt that telling her would almost certainly cause him to lose her. He quickly distracted himself from the idea, turning his attention to the explaining that he would have to do when he returned to the rink.

Kevin and Erin landed in Vancouver, picked up their car, and headed straight for the Olsen's. Both were quiet, but comfortable with the silence at the end of their trip. As they pulled into the driveway, they saw Neely, the Olsens' boxer-lab cross, sitting at the window, begrudgingly sharing his lookout spot with Tory. She quickly disappeared from the window to run to the door. When the door opened, Tory jumped up, arms outstretched to be caught by Kevin. Erin joined in for a family hug.

The whole Olsen family came to the door to greet them. Their collective expression tipped Kevin to the fact that Erin had shared the news of Cormie passing with Kate over the phone. Only Tory and the youngest of the Olsens, Bethany, seemed unaffected by the news.

Tory climbed down from Kevin, in order to give hugs to all of her hosts. Kate hugged Kevin, then asked what everyone else was wondering. "How are you holding up, Kev?"

"I've been better, but I'm doing okay," he replied with a nod.

"How about you, Erin?" Rick added.

"Hangin' in there," she answered, conjuring a tired smile.

Rick turned to Kevin and put his hand on his shoulder, unsure if Kevin would be comfortable with a hug. "Sorry to hear about Gord. He was a good man."

"The best," Kevin replied, looking appreciative of the sentiment.

Rick continued, "I hope it's okay, I talked to Bouche. He was pretty cool about it, so there's no need to worry about missed time."

Kevin looked instantly relieved, as he'd been dreading the possible consequences of his unexplained absence from practice the day before. "Thanks. I wasn't looking forward to having to deal with that."

"I didn't think so. That's why I went ahead and did it," Rick explained. "Are you coming to the morning skate?"

"Yeah. It'll probably do me some good to get on the ice," Kevin replied.

Rick nodded in agreement. Kate nudged him to prompt a question, "Oh . . . have you guys eaten?"

"Well we had a little bit on the plane but we'll probably find a little something at home," Erin replied.

"Well we thought that might be the case, so we ordered extra pizza in case you wanted to stay," Kate said hopefully.

Erin looked at Kevin and shrugged, her brow slightly raised, indicating that she saw no reason not to stay, but wanting him to make the decision.

"Well, we probably would have ordered in anyway," Kevin said, feeling hungry at the thought. "Sure, that sounds great."

"Should be here any minute." Kate said, looking at Kevin and sensing his hunger.

The two youngest girls scurried off to take advantage of the prolonged visit. Tory was content to stay, now that here parents were back. She'd received what she'd been missing as soon as they arrived, and was ready to play again.

The Wilkins and all of the Olsen's, even Meaghan, sat together in the living room, eating pizza and chatting. There was no talk of hockey or the trip to Calgary, instead it was mostly a recap of Tory's stay. Kayla, Bethany, and Tory argued playfully about the details. The chatter was broken occasionally by loud belly laughs from Tory, setting off the whole room with laughter.

Meaghan sat next to Erin, quietly confiding in her about boys, school, and soccer tryouts. She too had grown close to Erin during her pregnancy, having been old enough to understand some of what was going on. Erin listened attentively, glancing at Kate occasionally and smiling. Both Erin and Kate thought it was cute how Meaghan looked up to Erin.

"Poor old Neely got a raw deal when they started making dipping sauces for the crusts," Rick said with a laugh, looking at the dog. Everyone else laughed as they saw the panicked look on Neely's face, going frantically from chair to chair looking for offerings, and watching people devour the crusts to which he used to have dibs.

"Can I give him one of mine?" Kayla asked, moved by Neely's desperation.

"Yes, dear, but not at the table," Kate replied.

"I know. I know," Kayla insisted as Neely followed her to his bowl.

Erin noticed Kevin's eyes start to droop and quickly responded, "Well, this has been great, you guys, but we should really get this guy home to bed," she said, patting Kevin on the knee. It had been an awfully long day, especially for Kevin.

19

The next morning. Jamie Harris' office.

Kevin was alone in the office. Marcel Boucher was the only coach at the rink, reviewing an Edmonton game film in the next room. Kevin pulled the door shut and sat down. He read a number off of a long list above Harris' desk, then dialed. He fidgeted with a pen while he waited for an answer.

A woman with a thick southern accent finally spoke on the other end, "Dallas Stars Hockey Club. How may I direct your call?"

"Um, I'm . . . it's . . . it's Kevin Wilkins calling from Vancouver . . . um, I'm trying to reach Chuck Madison. Is he in?"

"I can try the locker room. Please hold."

As Kevin waited, the events of the Dallas game replayed in his head. The time that had elapsed since then seemed to shrink in his mind. It all felt as though it had just happened.

"Hello?" Madison's voice came across quietly. Kevin assumed that the receptionist had told him who was calling.

"Chuck?" Kevin prompted, just making sure.

"Yeah," Madison replied, waiting for an apology.

"It's Kevin Wilkins." Kevin stumbled over his words, unsure where to start.

"I know, Theresa upstairs told me."

"Oh . . . um . . ." *Just spill it, Wilk*, Kevin thought to himself. "I just wanted to tell you how sorry I am for what happened the other night." Madison didn't respond, apparently waiting for an explanation. Kevin continued, "My head was somewhere else completely, and when you knocked me over in the crease . . . something else just took over there for a second. Anyway, I wanted to say I'm sorry."

Madison finally responded, his voice softening slightly, "Well . . . I appreciate the call."

Kevin paused for a second, then added to his apology, unsatisfied with his effort so far, "I don't blame you for being pissed off. You have every right to be. But you're one of the last people that I would ever want to do that to," Kevin's words accelerated, now letting his thoughts come out fluidly, "I love the way you play. I have a huge amount of respect for you as a player. I mean, I really can't tell you how it happened. I'm not even sure myself. All I can say is . . . I wish more than anything that it hadn't."

"Thanks, Kevin. It helps to hear that," Madison said in a genuine tone that finally liberated Kevin from his uneasiness. At that moment, Kevin took on a whole new respect for Chuck Madison, not as a player, but as a person. Most players probably wouldn't have taken the call, except to retaliate verbally. Madison held his tongue, listened, and, by all indications, had forgiven the brutal attack that he had sustained.

Then he caught Kevin off guard. "Listen, Kevin, while I've got you on the phone, I was talking to Marshall, just a couple of minutes ago." Kevin had played with Dallas forward, Marshall Rourke, in Saskatoon. "I'm sorry to hear about Gord McCormack. Marshall said you two were pretty close."

"Yeah . . . we were. Thanks." Kevin kept his response short, feeling a wave of emotion from the day before hit him unexpectedly.

Madison sensed that he'd triggered something in Kevin, then hurried to let him off the phone. "Kevin we're about to hit the ice here. I should get going."

"Oh, of course, you're later than us." Kevin said, snapping out of his thoughts.

"Thanks though, Kevin. It was good of you to call," Madison added, feeling far more compassionate than he could possibly have anticipated, under the circumstances.

"Thanks, Chuck. Good luck in the first round," Kevin offered.

"You too." Madison responded, closing the conversation.

Kevin sat quietly for a moment then got up and walked to the locker room. He noticed someone walking out of the locker room, towards the treatment room, but couldn't tell who it was. Then his attention shifted to the front of his stall. There was a card and a tiny wreath, decorated with dried flowers and a ribbon. It struck him as a perfect gift to match his sentiment; why give a grieving person live flowers that will die in a few days? He figured it was the kind of thoughtful gift that only Kate would think of. He felt appreciative of Kate and Rick's friendship as he opened the card, expecting to see their names inside. The front of the card was white, framing a small picture of a setting sun. Then he looked inside the card and read:

We're very sorry about your loss.
Our deepest condolences.

Vladimir and Natasha

Both had signed the card, and Kevin could tell that the message was in Vladimir's writing. He sat back in his stall, feeling even more humbled than he had on the phone with Chuck Madison. For a moment, he sat in sadness, reflecting again on his loss. Then his reflections broadened, marveling at how his world suddenly looked so different. The events of the past week had shaken him, but strangely he was starting to settle back to a clear focus. A focus that placed Erin and Tory at the center. A focus that protected a special place for his lost friend and the wisdom that Cormie had offered. And perhaps most remarkably, his new perspective was conspicuously void of envy and resentment with respect to his teammate, Vladimir Koshenko. He laughed to himself as he thought of it, then sighed, ashamed of his former mindset.

Kevin changed into some workout clothes. He walked into the training facility, grabbed the T.V. remote, got on a stationary bike, and started to pedal. The morning edition of Sports Center showed still photos of Kevin and Erin leaving the hospital, followed by a picture of Cormie and some old footage of him and Kevin in Saskatoon. The story speculated about the relationship between McCormack's illness and Kevin's volatile behaviour in Dallas, replaying the footage of the hit.

Kevin felt unaffected by the infringement on his privacy, used to the lack of boundaries respected by the media. The Dallas footage didn't bother him either, as he finally felt that he had put the incident to rest. But the photo of Cormie elicited simultaneous sadness and fondness, still hurting about the loss, but feeling appreciative of all that Cormie had been to him.

But Kevin was tired of feeling and flicked through the channels as he sped up on the bike, finally settling for an aerobics program, not for inspiration, but rather for its aesthetic appeal. He muted the T.V. and settled into his ride, turning up the resistance and welcoming the slightly flushed feeling followed by sweat beading on his forehead.

Vlad Koshenko walked in with an ice pack on his shoulder and, without speaking, climbed onto the bike beside Kevin's. Kevin looked across and held out his fist. Vlad tapped it with his own fist and Kevin tapped him back, looking him in the eyes. "Thanks, Shenks." Vlad nodded in acknowledgement and leaned over onto the handle bars of his bike, spinning easily to loosen up his legs for his pre-practice stretch.

Being on the ice again felt different to Kevin. There was an easiness to it, a fluidity. He felt free, as if something had been lifted from his shoulders. The weight of the game, that he had carried previously, now seemed absurd in relation to the stuff that made up the last few days. He still sensed the tension in some of the players that he himself had felt just days earlier. The pressure from coaches. The pressure from the media. The pressure from the organization to perform. The pressure conjured from within each athlete to live up to personal standards. He saw it in Conrad Soles, who would be playing in his place during the suspension. He saw a tightness in goaltender, Mark Dorsey, who one sports writer had labelled 'unable to win the big games'. He even noticed a seriousness in Billy Morrison, who could normally be counted on to loosen things up.

Kevin saw things that he hadn't noticed before. Never before had he allowed himself to consciously admire Vladimir Koshenko's ability. The grace and efficiency of his stride. The precision of his movements. The delicate touch of his passes. Sheer mastery of the art of the game.

Kevin had noticed Rick's attention to the 'working class' aspects of the game before. He had tried to add them to his own game. But now, for the first time, Kevin noticed that Rick brought himself as a father to the ice. The patience with which he coached the younger players. The composure that he modeled for his teammates after mistakes. The nonverbal communication of his role as the 'alpha male'. His efforts to make sure that he treated everyone equally, the way he would at home if he were dishing the dessert.

But above all, Kevin noticed himself. He felt the strength of his stride that he had maximized in his off-season training, the rush of moving at top speed. He felt the puck on his stick and the exhilaration of handling it as if it were attached. He felt the satisfaction of a perfectly placed pass, not when it reached its target, but the moment it left his stick. He felt the power and precision of his shot, whether it was stopped or not. And he felt his place in the flow of the game, the synchronous movement of teammates, moving together with purpose, as if choreographed.

After practice, Kevin stayed to shoot around at one end of the rink. All three goalie's had left, but he was content to shoot on the empty net. Vlad Koshenko skated to the corner and started flipping passes to Kevin in front of the net. Kevin one-timed each pass heavily into the net, unphased by the occasional misfire. Both men fished the pucks out of the net, tapping them back into the corner. Vlad took his turn slapping one-timers into the empty net. When all the pucks were in the net, Kevin skated to the blueline and raised his stick, signaling for Vlad to pass him some pucks. Both players practiced deflecting slapshots from the blueline into the net. Kevin marveled at Vlad's skill, picking pucks easily out of the air. Kevin smiled as he watched his linemate put on a clinic in front of the net. Kevin and Vlad collected the pucks together, tossing them into a bucket. No words were spoken. None needed to be. The two Vancouver superstars had finally bonded, two games from their first playoff appearance in five years.

20

GM Place, Vancouver.

High above the ice, Kevin sat in the press box, his hands pressed together in front of his face. Edmonton was leading his team 4-1, midway through the third period. The Canucks' opportunity to move two points ahead of Edmonton into sole possession of sixth place was slipping away quickly. At 3-1, Kyle Kopp had pinched on a Vancouver rush, the pass by Billy Morrison had been tipped past him, resulting in a two-on-one rush the other way. Grady Shewchuk of the Oilers used his winger as a decoy and snapped a shot over the shoulder of Dorsey for the fourth goal.

Mark Dorsey was rattled, looking over at the bench at every whistle, wondering if there would be a change, indeed hoping that he'd be relieved from his misery. All four goals had beaten him cleanly, no deflections or screens. Marcel Boucher refused to take him out, hoping instead that a few good saves might salvage Dorsey's confidence. He also worried that pulling Dorsey would send the message that the towel was being thrown in.

Kevin wondered to himself why a goaltender switch had not been made, but only for a moment, as he knew the reason. Boucher was nothing if he was not stubborn. This was his silent demand for Mark Dorsey to fight back, to show some resilience, and he was not going to bend. Boucher and Dorsey had had this discussion before. But Dorsey was a creature of habit, maintaining in his own mind that his confidence had a threshold beyond which he could not recover. He believed that after a certain point, the best thing for him was to be pulled and regroup for his next outing. But Boucher continued to look everywhere but at him, leaving Dorsey to battle his own demons.

On the bench, most of the faces provided the game summary. They were being beaten in every aspect of the game, in their home rink. The Oilers had outscored, out-shot, out-hit, and out-hustled them for fifty minutes. Vlad Koshenko's play digressed with every failed attempt by Conrad Soles to keep pace with the top line. All of the defensemen had been banged up all night, even Kyle Kopp who was usually an elusive target for opposing forecheckers. The only bright spot was the play of their captain, Rick Olsen, who had scored his twentieth of the season to make it 3-1 and give the Canucks a ray of hope. But Shewchuk's goal less than a minute later had almost completely deflated them.

The more time that passed, the more uncomfortable Kevin felt, sitting helplessly in the press box. He was finished feeling guilty towards Chuck Madison; that, at least, had been put to rest. Now he felt badly for his teammates, who might have been in a completely different game were it not for his suspension. Kevin wished for a moment that he could go back and change the past, then realized that had it not been for the events in Dallas, he would not have reconnected with Cormie. Subsequently, the shift that his life was taking, back to his family, back to his values, back to himself, would not be taking place. He quickly changed his mind about his wish.

Kevin reflected on what he was feeling, as if stepping outside of himself for a moment. He felt guilty. Why? Because he acted selfishly out of anger and hurt his team. Perhaps it was a good thing that he felt this way. It certainly made him want never to do something like this again. And what would it take for him not to feel it? He couldn't blame the league. He felt the punishment was appropriate. He couldn't blame Madison. He did nothing to deserve it. So what would take that guilty feeling away? He would have to lose his commitment and sense of responsibility to his teammates. He was not willing to do that. His team mattered to him. That fact made his experience of the game more meaningful. More worthwhile. Yes, he had decided. He would just sit and feel uncomfortable, feel guilty. The alternative was not an option.

And it was uncomfortable. The Canucks were in a tough spot. A loss tonight would put them two points back of Edmonton. Even a win against Anaheim wouldn't move them back ahead. They would be tied, but Edmonton had more wins. A loss tonight would lock them into eighth place.

So what would that mean? The seventh place team would play Colorado, a team that they had beaten three times this season. The eighth place team would play St. Louis, the top team in the league, ten points ahead of the next closest team. They had dominated the regular season, and their games against Vancouver were no exception. The Canucks had managed only a tie in four meetings between the two teams, and were shut out twice. The team was definitely in a tough spot. And Kevin sat idly by, unable to help them.

The team's play continued to deteriorate, giving up scoring chances each time they gambled to create opportunities in the offensive zone. A miscommunication led to two defensemen joining the offensive rush. A shot was fired wide of the net and was cleared out off of the boards. Two Oiler forwards raced away with the puck. Matteus Krohn, the speedy Vancouver winger, raced back in time to catch Marcus Lareau, the forward who awaited the pass.

The forward with the puck slid it over to Lareau who was fighting off Krohn's hook. Krohn yanked hard with his stick, twisting Lareau sideways and off balance. Mark Dorsey slid across the crease, his pad outstretched, anticipating the shot. Krohn and Lareau were tangled up and unable to divert their course. They crashed heavily into Dorsey, knocking him backwards into the net. The crowd voiced their disapproval, despite the role that Krohn played in initiating the collision.

As Krohn and Lareau slowly got to their feet from on top of the Canuck netminder, Kevin noticed Dorsey moving his pads from side to side, in obvious pain. The crowd hushed as they realized that Dorsey was injured. Rick Olsen skated alongside the trainer, Tony Paxton, steadying him as he raced to tend to Dorsey. For several minutes, Paxton stood over Dorsey, assessing the injury. Eventually, Dorsey was helped to his feet and glided slowly to the bench. His left hand held his right arm, trying to support it. His shoulders appeared to be badly misaligned, with his left one sunken inches below his right.

Kevin was fairly sure he knew the diagnosis, even from the press box. Dorsey had dislocated his shoulder. Kevin squirmed in his seat as he imagined Paxton popping it back into place in the locker room. He'd never had it done himself, but had seen it enough times to understand just how painful a procedure it was.

Then Kevin's attention turned to the net where rookie goaltender, Stephane Oullett, was warming up. Oullett had dressed in place of veteran backup, Jack Simmons, who was nursing a sore groin. With only six minutes left to play, Krohn in the penalty box for hooking, the outcome of the game seemed to be decided. Many of the fans were headed for the exits, trying to beat the rush. But Kevin and his teammates now watched with renewed curiousity. Oullett had come up from the AHL affiliate after almost single handedly leading his team to an upset in their first round of the playoffs. But a strong performance tonight might make Boucher's decision, about who would assume the number one role in Dorsey's absence a difficult one.

Six minutes and eleven saves later, Oullett had made a fairly strong statement about his readiness to play in the league. He would most likely get the nod against Anaheim, but Boucher would have to see Oullett in a whole game before he would decide about the starter in game one versus St. Louis.

At the buzzer, the Vancouver situation had taken on a grim shade. They were going into the playoffs against the most dominant team in the league. They would do so without their starting goalie, with either a rookie or an ailing veteran in his place. And for the first three games, they would be without their second leading scorer, Kevin Wilkins, whose presence was clearly missed in the chemistry of the top line. Without a win on Saturday against Anaheim, they would also be riding a three game losing streak into the playoffs.

Kevin headed down to the locker room to console his teammates. On his way down the corridor, he saw local newspaper reporter, Al Frank. Frank was a self-professed 'tell-it-like-it-is' sports writer, which Kevin interpreted as an excuse to be as big an asshole as you want in the name of hard-nosed journalism. He pretended not to see him, but knew there was not much chance of getting by unnoticed. With his head down, walking quickly, he thought he'd gotten by when he heard Frank's voice.

"Hey Wilk! You got a second, buddy?" Kevin didn't like the reporter calling him Wilk as if they were friends. He didn't like 'buddy' much either. Al Frank had a habit of acting like one of the boys, then ripping them to shreds in his column. But Kevin made a split-second decision to try to be diplomatic.

"Sure Al, but just a second, alright?"

Frank nodded as he fiddled with his tape recorder. "Any comment on the game tonight?" Frank asked fishing for dissention.

Don't give him anything to run with, Wilk, Kevin thought to himself. 'Well, it's a tough loss obviously, considering the playoff picture, but Edmonton was really on their game tonight. They moved the puck extremely well. They took the body hard. And their big guns were blazing."

"While yours weren't," Frank added pretending to follow Kevin's train of thought.

Shit! Walked right into that one, he chastised himself in his head. "Our guns will be firing just fine in St. Louis. Solesy will have another game to get used to playing on the first line and they won't even miss me. He's a big strong power forward. He's tailor-made for playoff hockey." Kevin played his response back in his head, looking for ways it could be turned around.

"How's it feel watching from up top?" Frank continued, not bothered by the stupidity of his question.

"It's tough, but I made my own bed. That outburst in Dallas was selfish and inexcusable, and this is the consequence. Obviously, I can't take it back. All I can do is make sure I'm ready to go in game four." *Nowhere to go from there.*

"Have you had any contact with Madison, since the incident?" Frank asked.

"We spoke this morning. He was more forgiving than I could ever have hoped. He's one classy individual." Kevin now felt confident that he could handle Frank's questions, and he knew what the next one would be.

"There's been some speculation that Gord McCormack's condition may have led to your volatile behaviour in Dallas. Any comment?"

"For the record, I didn't learn about his condition until after the Dallas game. Gord McCormack spent his coaching career teaching respect and discipline to his players. My hit on Chuck Madison went against everything that Gord was about. I'm ashamed and embarrassed by the incident and will not make excuses about it, only a promise that I'll never do anything like that again. I've gotta run, Al."

"Thanks Wilk," Frank offered as Kevin turned to go. The dissatisfaction in his voice was encouraging to Kevin. He must not have given him much to go on. But almost everything he said was true, minus the bit about Conrad Soles. Kevin thought that one of the skilled second liners should have moved up. He felt that Boucher was mistakenly assuming that the line needed a power forward. Conrad Soles was no Kevin Wilkins. Kevin knew it. Vladimir and Billy knew it. And now twenty thousand Vancouver fans and countless other CTV Sportsnet viewers knew it.

Down in the locker room, Kevin went straight to Mark Dorsey. "How bad, Doc?" He called Dorsey Doc because of his 'MD' initials. Dorsey seemed to like it.

"Bad," Dorsey replied, with a sour look on his face. Dorsey shook his head and rolled his eyes, then looked back at Kevin and added, "I shouldn't have even fuckin' been out there."

Kevin didn't really want to give Dorsey an excuse to blame Boucher for the injury. It was bad luck. Boucher couldn't have known it would happen. Instead, he patted Dorsey gently on the back, careful not to shake his shoulder. "Tough luck, Doc. Just get better quick." Dorsey didn't reply.

Kevin sat down next to Rick, who sat in a trance, still wearing most of his gear. "Looked like a tough one out there," Kevin prompted.

"Yeah," Rick answered still looking straight ahead. Then he finally looked over at Kevin, "Tougher to watch, I bet," he added, smiling faintly.

Kevin nodded, laughing under his breath. "Think Soederberg should have moved up?" Kevin asked. Lars Soederberg was a crafty second line winger with great offensive touch. The knock on him was his speed, but he made up for a lot with his game smarts, and, in actual fact, he was faster than people gave him credit for.

Rick again stared straight ahead, processing the question, then nodded surely. "But Solesy wasn't the only weak link tonight. We'd better crank it up for Saturday. We need some positives going into St. Louis. The memorial service on Saturday?" Rick asked, flipping the focus.

Kevin nodded, looking at his feet. He was amazed at Rick's habit of always focusing on other people's problems. *Who helps him with his own issues? Kate, of course*, Kevin remembered, answering his own question.

"Well, I'll be thinking of you . . . until game time," Rick said, smiling and giving Kevin a playful shove with his forearm. "Hell, if Solesy plays the way he did tonight, I'll be thinking of you all game," Rick laughed, careful not to be overheard.

Kevin stood up, still laughing quietly. He held out his hand to Rick and they shook. "See ya tomorrow, Olse."

"Hi to Erin," Rick added.

Kevin looked back at him and smiled. It felt good hearing Rick say it without sarcasm. It felt even better that he couldn't wait to see her. "Same to Kate," Kevin replied.

As Kevin left the building, he remembered what Cormie had said about leaving the game at the rink. An important loss carries with it a heaviness that many players take home with them. Even the ones that don't dress. But Kevin took a deep breath, and slowly let out both the air and the heaviness as he walked to his truck. *I hope she's still up*, he thought to himself as he pulled out of his spot.

Erin sat on the bed, watching T.V., but not paying much attention to it. She knew Kevin would be home soon. She had made a pot of tea for herself and had the fixings for a fruit smoothie on the cupboard for Kevin. She reflected on how long it had been since she was excited about Kevin coming home. It had been a while.

When she heard the garage door, she scurried downstairs to pour her tea and blend Kevin's smoothie. He heard the blender as he came in and knew what she was up to. He walked in and hugged her from behind. She turned off the blender and reached over her shoulders to hug him back, smiling. *He'll probably want to debrief the game a little*, she thought. "Tough one to watch, eh?" she started, giving him the opening, and turning to face him.

Kevin shrugged. "Yeah, no point in reliving it, I guess," he said, as he poured his smoothie into a large glass. "Thanks for the drink," he said, changing the subject.

"You're welcome," she replied, looking a little stunned that he seemed to be done talking about hockey for the evening.

"So what did you two do tonight?" Kevin continued.

"Well, it was so hot all day we decided to go swimming. And Tory dog-paddled the whole width of the pool without her water wings," Erin stated grandly, sitting up straight in her chair and beaming with pride.

"Get outta here!" Kevin replied, his eyes widening.

"Yep," Erin said, laughing, "I even held out my hand twice and got in trouble for it. "No Mommy!" Erin exclaimed in her best little girl voice.

"That's awesome!" Kevin said, laughing along with her.

Kevin and Erin sat up chatting, mostly about Tory. They laughed, smiled, and reminisced a little, sipping their drinks, and touching each other's feet under the table. To both of them, it felt easy, it felt real, but most of all, it just felt right. Occasionally, Kevin's thoughts drifted to the secret that he still harboured from his wife. But then he would return to the moment that he was in, resolving that he would eventually tell her. But for tonight, this was nice. Too nice to be disturbed.

21

Saturday. Bernard-Foster Funeral Home, Calgary.

Joyce Mitchell, the minister who would perform the service explained to Kevin when she would call on him to speak. She showed him how to adjust the microphone, which was set for her, a full foot too low for him. It was still early. The guests would not start to arrive for another half hour or so. Erin and Tory had found the playroom, a wise addition to the facility. Most young children did not fully understand the concept of death, much less the ceremony attached to it.

Kevin sat alone in one of the pews, rehearsing his speech in his head. He was nervous. Much more nervous than he'd ever been for a hockey game. As he reflected on the memories that he drew from in writing the eulogy, he was able to calm himself, distracted by the pleasantness of his recollections.

Gord had been cremated as per his wishes. He wanted to be remembered alive, not made to look like he was still alive. Kevin was glad. Two open casket funerals for his grandparents made him feel the same way. The memory of their bodies that 'almost' looked like them left Kevin uncomfortable with the whole process. Instead, a bronze urn sat on a table at the front, along with a photo mosaic that Lorna's sister had helped her to prepare.

Kevin heard the doors open slowly, followed by Joyce Mitchell's voice, "Hello, Lorna."

"Hi Joyce. Is Kevin here yet?" Lorna sounded more composed than Kevin thought she would. He wondered if he would cry before she did.

"Yes, he's in there. And the girls found the toys down the hall," Joyce added warmly.

"Oh, good! I wasn't sure if Tory would be along this time," Lorna said, pleasantly surprised.

Kevin had walked to the entrance of the chapel to meet her. She smiled reassuringly, when she saw him. He bent down to hug her and she hugged him back firmly, then gave him a kiss on the cheek.

"How are you doing?" Kevin asked, looking her right in the eyes.

Lorna nodded as she spoke, "Okay so far. How about you?"

"Pretty nervous actually. I'm not sure if I'm gonna be able to hold it together," he replied in complete honesty.

"If you don't, you don't, Kevin. And that's okay. If it were Gord at your memorial, he'd be through a whole box of tissue by now." she said, managing a laugh. Kevin and Lorna stood looking at each other for a moment. Both started to well up when Tory appeared below them. She tugged on Kevin's finger, awaiting an introduction.

"Do you remember Tory, Lorna?" Kevin asked, pulling himself together.

"Of course, but you're almost all grown up now," she replied, looking down at Tory. "And you look just lovely in that dress," she continued, bending over and touching Tory on the arm.

Tory smiled and twirled her skirt shyly. Then she looked at her mother for reassurance and then back at Lorna. "Sorry for your loss,

Mrs. McCormack." Tory offered quietly, as if rehearsed, her r-sound charmingly absent.

Lorna knelt down and hugged her. "Thank you, dear. That's very sweet of you." Tory hugged back, eyes closed and her face resting on Lorna's shoulder, as if she was hugging her Grandma. Erin choked back her tears, moved by the moment. Kevin watched Tory, and found a sense of peace for the first time since they had arrived for the service.

The hour that followed was quite pleasant for Kevin, reuniting with old teammates and coaches, even fans and community folks from Saskatoon. He was encouraged by the huge number of people that had come to pay their respects to Gord McCormack. He certainly had touched a lot of lives. Kevin's butterflies returned when he realized he'd have to get up in front of all of them and speak.

Kevin sat at the front of the chapel with Erin and Tory during the service. He felt a little uncomfortable with all the talk about Jesus and God by the minister, recalling that Cormie was not particularly religious. Then he reminded himself where he was and decided not to let it bother him. It was clear that the McCormacks knew Joyce Mitchell. She spoke of him as a friend would, more than as a servant of God. By the time she was finished, Kevin felt good about her involvement.

"Now I'd like to ask Kevin Wilkins to come up and say a few words," Joyce said, startling Kevin back to his task. He suddenly felt flushed when he felt the eyes of the congregation turn to him. His legs felt weak under him as he stepped to the lectern. He fumbled with the microphone, trying to adjust it. Joyce Mitchell stepped over to help him adjust it, then touched him on the hand and whispered "you'll be fine".

Kevin looked out at the crowd, noticing that several people stood at the back, and even more were in the hallway outside of the chapel, unable to squeeze in. Kevin took a deep breath, glanced down at the Erin for comfort, then spoke softly into the microphone.

"Cormie would laugh himself silly if he could see me shaking up here." The congregation chuckled, giving Kevin a little bit of confidence.

"When I first went to Saskatoon, I used to get really nervous before games. Cormie told me the players that perform best under pressure are usually the ones that imagine they're just playing on the pond with their buddies. So if it's okay with all of you, I'll be picturing everyone in touques and mitts for the next few minutes." More laughter but Kevin knew the tough part was yet to come.

"When most people picture a hockey coach, they see a guy who is hard-nosed and . . . usually angry. But people who knew Cormie know that he didn't fit that mould. That's not to say that he never got upset, but the kinds of things that he got upset about can tell you a lot about him. He got upset when a player quit on himself. He got upset when players didn't treat each other with respect. He got upset when players swore when there were kids around. He got upset when players swore when Lornie was around." More laughter, even from Lorna.

"But the things that really upset Cormie usually had to do with himself. He got upset with himself when players felt that they hadn't been treated fairly. He got upset with himself when players fell behind in their studies when they were on the road. He was too much of a softy to crack the whip. He got really upset when he had to cut players from a team. He hated that part of his job." Many heads nodded.

"And while these things help to understand him a little, the things that made Cormie happy tell the story even better. He was happy when he saw that look in a player's eye that said 'I've got it'. He was happy on the bus, sitting in the back listening to players tell dirty jokes. He used to sit back there and laugh until he cried, but wouldn't tell any because he didn't want to corrupt us. He was happy when we played well, regardless of whether we won or not. He was happy when the bus pulled in because he couldn't wait to see Lornie." Lorna smiled, tears already streaming down her cheeks. "In short, he was happy when the people in his life were happy.

"Cormie was proud of lots of things. He was proud of players that reached their potential. He was proud when his players refused to give up, regardless of whether they were successful or not. He was proud when players did well in school. He didn't miss many graduations. He was proud when players found girls that they really cared about. He's been to his fair share of weddings too.

"But what I'll remember most is the way that Cormie loved. He loved the game, the pure simple joys of it. He loved his players like they were his children. He loved his wife, as much as anyone that I have ever known." Lorna began to sob, leaning into her sister. Kevin had to look away from her to keep from breaking down himself.

"And now that I have to say goodbye, I think the best way to put it into words is to say how I feel. I'm upset that I don't always live my own life the way that Cormie taught me how to. I'm upset that . . ." Kevin had welled up and was trembling, "I'm upset that I never told Cormie just how much he meant to me." Kevin's voice cracked as he fought to continue. He took a deep breath and let it out slowly.

"But I'm happy that he packed so much living into his life, even though it was cut short. I'm happy that he was there to see me graduate, that he was the best man at my wedding, and that he got to meet my little girl." Kevin pointed to Tory in the front pew. "I'm happy that I got to spend so much time with such a wonderful man". Kevin leaned away from the podium and shook as he sobbed quietly. Erin cried with him from her seat. Then he took another breath, wiped his nose with a tissue, and continued.

"And now I'm proud of Cormie for touching the lives of so many people, only a fraction of which are crammed in here today. I'm proud because I know that the lessons he taught will live on for generations to come. I'm proud to say that Gord McCormack . . . was my best friend.

"Now I'm learning to love the game the way that Cormie did. I love my wife and my daughter, with all my heart, the only way Cormie knew how to love. And even though it took me this long to say it . . ." Kevin clenched his teeth, determined to finish, "Cormie . . . I will always love you."

Kevin stepped down to Lorna, dropped to his knees and embraced her, both of them sobbing loudly. Erin moved around Kevin to hug him, also sobbing. Tory nestled her way into the huddle, now crying a little herself, although she didn't fully understand why.

Throughout the chapel, people dug tissues out of their purses and pockets, moved by Kevin's words as they resonated so powerfully with their own experiences. Joyce Mitchell stepped up to the podium, adjusted the microphone and spoke, looking down at Kevin, "Beautifully said, Kevin."

22

Kevin's eulogy seemed to be healing for many of the people at the service. Many who had fought their own tears finally gave in when Kevin's emotions were so visible. Not surprisingly, the congregation included many ex-players whose lives had been touched by Gord McCormack in similar ways. Kevin gave license to their grief. For a few short minutes, the 'big boys don't cry' pretense was dropped, and everyone was able to feel the loss fully.

Kevin thought he'd feel embarrassed if he cried at the service. Instead he felt relief. He needed to cry. It made no sense to pretend he felt strong and unaffected. He had lost a friend and a father figure. His tears were a tribute to the relationship that he had lost in body, but still embraced in spirit.

Kevin had never cried in front of Tory. But he was so absorbed by the moment that he could not edit his expression on her behalf. He had long believed that the father needed to be strong and composed, 'unshakeable'. His view was changing. He was glad that she could see him cry. Because she would see his strength in years to come, and would come to understand that the strong can cry. In fact, sometimes they must cry, if they are to draw strength from the past.

As for Erin, she had demonstrated vividly one of the qualities that Kevin loved most about her. She felt what he felt, seemingly in the same intensity. She made it her business to go inside the people she cared about and understand what they loved and why. That way, whenever they were happy, she felt it with them. Whenever they were sad, she felt that too. But whatever they felt, they never felt it alone. This day, Kevin felt sad, but could not remember a time that he felt closer to his wife, his daughter, or himself.

Although very crowded, the reception had an intimate feel to it. People laughed, smiled and sighed as they recounted their own experiences with Cormie and each other. Over the speakers played a disk of Cormie's favourite songs that Lorna and her sister, Joan, had tearfully compiled while they were assembling the photo mosaic. Kevin smiled as he heard the voice of Ra McGuire of Trooper making a particularly poignant point:

> *"We're here for a good time, not a long time.*
> *So have a good time, the sun can't shine everyday."*

Kevin felt a wave of contentment come over him. This is how Cormie would have wanted it. This would have made him happy. Erin leaned over and gave Kevin a squeeze. She knew what he was thinking.

Then Kevin suddenly recognized a young man making his way through the crowd towards him. He was handsome and athletic looking, but smaller than Kevin. He wore small round glasses, and his brown hair hung down, almost to his eyes. Kevin was excited to see him but felt unprepared, as he had intended to reunite on his own terms.

"Brad," he exclaimed, his eyes wide. "What are you doing here?"

"I heard about Coach McCormack and thought maybe this would be a good chance to see you. I hope that's okay," he replied cautiously.

"Yeah . . . yeah, of course," Kevin assured him, pulling him in for a hug. Kevin embraced Brad tightly, wondering for a moment if he had ever *really* 'hugged' him. Brad seemed surprised but pleased with Kevin's response. Both men had much to say, and issues to resolve with each other, but this initial response was telling about how those discussions would go. They had hurt each other, but discovered in an instant that the damage was reparable, something neither would have guessed until this moment. They missed each other.

As they hugged, Kevin realized that Brad had not come alone. Behind him was an older woman, slight in frame, whose eyes had welled up as she watched her two sons embrace.

"Mom," Kevin said softly, suddenly feeling small and childlike.

"Hi Kev." Susan Wilkins said, looking antsy as she awaited her own hug. "We thought maybe you could use a little extra family today," she said, sniffling. Kevin grabbed her gave her a long bear hug.

"Thanks for coming," Kevin whispered as he hugged.

Erin hugged Brad hello, relieving him of his uncertainty of whether or not that was appropriate. "Nice to see you, Brad," she offered, reassuringly.

"You too, Erin." Brad replied shyly. "It's been quite a while." It had been four years. Erin remembered Brad as an 18 year-old kid who seemed to possess a maturity that eluded his peers. Now he stood before her as a man, similar to, but distinct from Kevin. She smiled warmly at him, hoping he understood that the long time they hadn't been in touch with him was not her choice.

Then Erin hugged Kevin's mother. "Hi Susan. Good to see you." Kevin's mom had insisted that Erin call her by her first name, from when they first met. She still preferred to be seen as a friend rather than as an in-law.

Tory stood below her grandma with arms outstretched. "Graaamaaa," she exclaimed, as though she'd been waiting for some time.

"Hello Tory, sweetheart!" Susan replied, lifting Tory up onto her waist. Tory clung to her grandma, smiling widely, anticipating a longer visit than it was going to be.

Brad stepped around so that Tory could see him. "We've never met before, Tory. I'm . . ."

Tory cut him off before he could finish. "You're my Uncle Brad. Grandma showed me your pictures." Brad paused, a little surprised then half-laughed, not quite sure how to respond. Tory buried her head in her grandma's shoulder, still smiling. She had surprised herself with her forwardness and now felt a little timid.

Kevin looked away uncomfortably, suddenly overrun with guilt. His only brother was meeting his firstborn for the first time when she was three and a half, a decision that he had consciously made because of hurt feelings. When Brad glanced at Kevin, Erin saw no signs of resentment, but she did sense that he was expecting an apology at some point.

Erin rushed to fill the pause. "Tory, guess where your Uncle Brad goes to school." She prompted, remembering that they had talked about this before.

Tory looked stumped and offered a guess quietly, "Medicine Hat?"

"No sweetie, remember when we were looking at the pictures at Grandma's?" Erin said, hoping to demonstrate that Tory had some knowledge of the uncle she hadn't met. "Sssss," she prompted.

Tory's eyes widened quickly, "Saskatoon! Where you met Daddy!" she blurted out, excited by the recollection.

"That's pretty good, Tory," Brad said reassuringly, more for Erin than Tory. "And that's where your dad played for Mr. McCormack," he continued, respecting the event that had brought them all together.

Kevin finally overcame the awkwardness and spoke. "Um, maybe we could all have lunch together. We don't fly out until 6:30."

"Well . . . we were sort of hoping that we could steal you guys away. But only if you don't have commitments here already." Susan said hopefully.

"I'll talk to Lorna, but I suspect that she'll insist we spend the time with you guys . . . she's like that," Kevin assured her.

"Well, Brad, you seem to know lots of the boys here. Why don't you stay and come with Kevin when he's ready. We'll get a table at the Earls near the airport. I can take the girls with me and pick up Carla from the mall," Susan suggested, making a spur of the moment decision to risk leaving her boys together.

"Carla?" Kevin and Erin asked simultaneously.

"Who's Carla?" Tory added for good measure.

"You'll see." Susan responded smugly. "But first I'd like to say a quick hello to Lorna." Susan and Lorna had often sat together at games in Saskatoon. While Susan knew Gord mostly by reputation, she knew first hand what kind of person Lorna was and was intensely appreciative of the support that she had provided to Kevin in Saskatoon.

"Oh, okay," Erin said, taking Tory by the hand, "she's just over there." She motioned with her head at Lorna across the room.

"Well, when are we meeting?" Kevin asked, feeling a little rushed.

"You'll get there when you get there, Kev. We've got lots to talk about. Don't worry about us," Susan said, touching both girls on their heads.

Kevin nodded, too drained to disagree. He looked at Erin as they walked away. She looked back at him and shrugged, but smiled easily, as if to assure him that the plan would work out fine.

"Good 'ole Mom, eh? Miss Spontaneous," Kevin said, turning his attention to Brad.

Brad nodded and laughed. "Yep. We were sitting at home with her last night and as soon as I mentioned that you'd be here today, she was on her way to the kitchen to fix snacks for the road," Brad explained, still laughing.

"Came up this morning?" Kevin asked, annoyed with himself for reverting to small talk.

"Yeah," Brad answered, feeling a little awkward himself.

"That's not a bad drive. It just takes about three hours, right?" Kevin continued.

"Three and a half . . . Mom drove." Both men laughed. It felt good to laugh together again.

Kevin's face went serious, as did Brad's. Brad knew Kevin was searching for the words to say something. He waited quietly.

"Man, I feel like an idiot now because I was gonna call you and didn't," Kevin finally got out. Brad smiled sympathetically. Kevin went on, "The truth is, I was pretty pissed off the last time we talked, and it's only been recently that I've considered the possibility that some of what you said might have been right."

"Well, I was pretty harsh, Kev. I could have been a lot more diplomatic," Brad replied, letting his brother off the hook a little.

"Yeah, but that's not really the point. I let four years slip away because of hurt feelings. That's just crap." Kevin insisted, looking annoyed with himself.

"Look, Kev," Brad tried to interject.

"Just let me finish, Brad. I've been thinking about what I wanted to say to you for a few days. I don't want to fuck it up." Kevin lowered his voice as he swore, not wanting to offend anyone nearby. "You made a decision for yourself and I didn't respect that. You didn't allow yourself to get all wrapped up in the hockey hoopla. I had a chance to talk to Cormie right before he died. He helped me to set some stuff right in my head. I've been a shitty brother for the last four years. Lately I've been a pretty shitty husband and teammate too. But all that is changing. I'm gonna make things right, one way or another." Brad looked concerned, wondering what all Kevin was referring to.

Kevin took a deep breath and let it out slowly. "And to start with, I'm sorry I haven't been in touch. I'm sorry you waited three and a half years to meet your niece. And I'm sorry I couldn't see that maybe we just wanted different things."

Brad waited a moment to make sure that Kevin was done. "Wow. Well, my turn. I let four years go by too. To tell you the truth, I didn't think we'd ever see eye to eye again. But a lot of the decisions I made were out of anger. Not that I regret going to U of S; it's worked out really well. But I was mad at the business. And I turned my back on it. But I also wrapped you up with it. And I'm sorry for that." He paused for a moment, then continued. "You probably didn't know this, but soon after Tory was born, Erin called, trying to get me to call you and reconcile. And I wouldn't. I was too stubborn."

Kevin started to smile, recalling a similar experience. "Yeah, she came at me pretty hard with the same thing, hormones a'blazin'." Both men laughed. There was a long pause, then Kevin's smile emerged again and he summed it all up, "What a couple of assholes." Again they both laughed, but now there was relief in their laughter. Kevin wrapped his long arms around his brother, "Ah, it's great to see you, little bro."

"You too . . . Big Wilk." Brad responded, smiling.

"Well, will wonders never cease?!" Lorna McCormack exclaimed as she witnessed their hug. "Gord will certainly be smiling down on this," she continued. "The Wilkins brothers back in the same room. How do you like that?" Lorna was neither capable nor willing to beat around the bush at this junction in her life.

"Yeah, it took too long, but we're back. Brad, do you remember Mrs. McCormack?" Kevin asked, remembering his manners.

"Sure, we had pizza when I came to see you in Sask." Brad recalled.

"Oh yeah, that's right." Kevin squinted, trying to recall. He remembered vaguely, but it was not the highlight to him that it had been to Brad.

"It sure was nice of you and your mom to come, Brad. But you two should probably go catch up with the girls," Lorna insisted, in trademark fashion.

"What did I tell you?" Kevin asked, looking at Brad. Then he turned to Lorna, placed his hands on her shoulders and kissed her on the cheek. "I'll be in touch. Take care of yourself, okay?"

Lorna kissed him back on the cheek and insisted, "Oh, I'll be fine, Kev. But thanks. You just take good care of your girls."

Kevin waved as they walked away. He noticed tears in the corners of Lorna's eyes, but she continued to smile. They looked like tears of happy sentiment, not of sorrow. At least that's what he hoped he saw.

23

It took the Wilkins boys several minutes to make it to the car. They were both considered celebrities in this crowd. Kevin more for his major junior days than his NHL accomplishments, and Brad for his recent exploits with the University of Saskatchewan Huskies, who also played in Saskatoon.

They climbed into Kevin's rental car. Kevin put the keys in the ignition, but didn't start it. Instead, he stared straight ahead, as if searching his memory, then turned to Brad and asked, "So who's Carla?"

Brad smiled, knowing that this was coming. "She's my fiancé," he said, leaving his older brother dangling. Kevin started the car and pulled out of the parking lot.

"Alright, spill it little brother. Tell me a story," Kevin insisted, trying to hide his excitement.

"Well, I was picking up a course last summer, so I was at the U. And when I went to work out after class, I walked by one of the Phys. Ed. classrooms and I saw her teaching a dance class."

"Oo, dancer's body?" Kevin inquired.

"Yeah."

"Nice."

Brad snickered at the interruption then continued, "Oh man, I was just spellbound. She was demonstrating a step, and just seemed to float across the floor. She was just so beautiful."

"You were smitten." Kevin clarified.

"Oh . . . big time. But it wasn't even a sexual thing. It was like watching a bird fly or a waterfall. I was just captivated. But then she totally busted me. She glanced towards the door and I was just totally mesmerized. I couldn't look away! I was like . . . such a loser. Anyway, she looked away, smiling a little, and when it finally registered that the class was laughing at me, I slinked away to the gym."

Kevin threw his head back, laughing. "Pretty smooth, little bro."

"Oh yeah. I was a regular Don Juan." Brad added, sharing in the laugh. "So off I go to the gym, tail between my legs. And then when I'm walking to my car, I see her standing on the sidewalk, looking around. So, the closer I get, the more nervous I get, and I'm trying to think of something to say. But when I got close enough, I was just rattled. I kept my head down and kept walking."

"Oh come on," Kevin said, in disbelief.

"No shit. That's what I did. But then I hear this little voice behind me. 'Excuse me.' And I turn around and she's looking at me. I still couldn't talk. I just pointed to my chest in disbelief."

"Deer in the headlights." Kevin added.

"Totally. Then she giggled and said she couldn't remember where she was parked. So I end up helping her find her car. And by that time I figured she was so unimpressed that I finally relaxed a little and could actually . . . you know, talk. And when we got to her car she thanked me and started to get in, then stood up and she goes, 'Are you around on Thursday'. And I'm like, 'yeah', as if I'd say no. So she goes, 'I'm teaching another class. Maybe I could buy you a juice after or something'. So I said 'that'd be great', and I'm walking away dumbfounded, wondering what she could possibly have seen in me."

Kevin couldn't take it anymore. "Brad, you're unbelievable! You're good looking, athletic. You're a friggin' genius in school. Why wouldn't girls like you?"

Brad shrugged, embarrassed by the praise. "Anyway, we met for a juice, and fought over who would pay. She's a pretty stubborn little thing. But then it became a standing Tuesday and Thursday date. And then, one Saturday, she invited me to a dance recital for the dance academy that she taught at. And it was pretty cool. Then after, we went for a walk along the river and talked about absolutely everything."

Kevin was very sentimental about walks along the Saskatchewan River. He flashed back in his head to his proposal to Erin on such a walk. Then he snapped out of it and returned his attention to Brad. "So did you kiss her?"

"She kissed me! She just got quiet all of a sudden, got up onto her tiptoes, and kissed me."

"Cool. Any tongue?"

"Kev . . ." Brad started, shaking his head.

"Sorry," Kevin quickly inserted.

"So anyway . . . I just melted. I fell head over heals in an instant. I love everything about this girl. She's smart. She's independent. She went away to New York to do a fine arts degree when she was seventeen. Then, on a whim, she leaves a teaching job in Ottawa to open a studio in Saskatoon with a friend that she met at school. She's petite and fit looking. And she's not drop dead gorgeous, but I just think she's so exotic looking. Her family is from Hungary. They moved here when she was ten. She didn't speak a word of English, but now, you have to listen carefully to hear her accent."

Kevin smirked, then asked, "So how long did it take you to tell her you were a hockey player?"

Brad smiled, acknowledging in his head that he hadn't intended to tell her for a long time, then answered, "Second date. She was relentless. She kept peppering me with questions. She wanted to know everything. But she had never seen a hockey game before."

"Shut up," Kevin barked in disbelief, his eyes widening.

"Nope," Brad giggled. "So she came to our home opener with her friend that she runs the academy with, and she absolutely loved it! I even had kind of a lousy game, but she didn't care. She just loved all the movement. She said I looked graceful on the ice. And she couldn't believe that two teams with opposite intentions could move so rhythmically together."

"Oh God." Kevin said, rolling his eyes.

"No, Kev. That was my initial response too. But then I saw what she saw. I can actually feel the flow of the game better than I ever could! I had the most fun playing this year that I've ever had. And I think that's part of it."

Kevin took the opportunity to open a new discussion. "So are you gonna go to the Columbus camp?" Brad looked at Kevin, surprised that he had heard about the offer. Kevin continued, "Oh, come on. You don't think I hear stuff? They're pretty high on you."

Brad shrugged, then explained. "Well, I applied to medicine at U of S, and if I get in, I'm for sure staying."

"And if you don't?" Kevin prompted.

"Then it's decision time. I can either go and give it a shot, or start a Masters in exercise physiology, then reapply. The prof that supervised my honours thesis said he'd love to have me." Brad went on, hoping that Kevin could see it his way.

"Oh, come on Brad! You can go back to school anytime!" Brad looked back at Kevin, not trying to hide his disappointment. Kevin dropped his shoulders and nodded, catching himself in the act. "Sorry, man. Sort of slipped back in time there for a second. You need to figure out what's best for you. I'm behind you, whatever you decide."

Brad's smile returned, "Thanks, Kev. That means a lot."

The car was quiet for a moment, then a smirk came over Kevin's face. He looked over at Brad through the corner of his eye, then said quietly, "I bet you'd make it in Columbus though." They both laughed. Brad shook his head at his brother, accepting that some things might never change.

As they pulled into the parking lot, Kevin started wondering what preconceptions Carla might already have about him, considering the only side that she would have heard. As if Kevin's thoughts were on a loud speaker, Brad sensed his apprehension and spoke, "Don't worry, Kev. Carla will take you as you are. She helped me to turn my attitude around and consider patching things up with you."

Kevin smiled faintly, a little embarrassed by his transparency. A week ago, he would have denied that he had any concerns. He was in a different place now. "Sounds like quite a catch, Brad."

As they spotted the girls at a corner table, Carla stood to greet them. She wore an orange sleeveless sun dress. Kevin figured she couldn't stand more than 5 foot 2. She looked muscular but slight, not more than a hundred pounds. Her skin was tight and lightly tanned. Her hair was died jet black and pulled back in a ponytail, with short bangs framing her thin face. She smiled widely as she reached up to hug Brad and give him a kiss on the cheek. He looked huge beside her.

Kevin stepped forward and held out his hand to shake. "Hi Carla, I'm Kevin."

She took his hand with both of her tiny hands and pulled him down to kiss him on the cheek. "Nice to finally meet you, Kevin." Erin watched gleefully. Kevin could tell she already loved Carla. He understood why. He felt simultaneously proud of Brad and a little self-conscious that he found his brother's fiancé so attractive. Brad could see it in his eyes but wasn't bothered. He understood that she seemed to have that affect on almost everybody.

The six of them sat for as long as they could until Kevin, Erin, and Tory had to go to make their flight. Brad offered to drive on the way back to Medicine Hat so that his mom could have a few margaritas; also so that they could be home inside of three hours. She told embarrassing childhood stories about Kevin and Brad. Erin, Carla, and Tory sat and laughed, Tory most of all. Kevin and Brad slunk down in their seats, rolling their eyes at the most embarrassing stories, but managed to laugh along, in spite of themselves.

Susan's ex-husband, Greg, was never mentioned, as if they had agreed not to mention him years ago. Both Erin and Carla knew why. They'd heard the stories in private before. Tory was none the wiser.

They talked about hockey, and dance, and Brad's honour's thesis. Susan updated them on all the gossip back in Medicine Hat. As they chatted, Carla watched Erin, wondering if she had a passion of her own. Clearly she loved being a mother, but Carla thought she seemed too interesting not to have other aspirations. But as she watched and listened to Tory, she understood a little better how other interests could be forgotten, at least for a little while.

24

On a plane starting its descent to Vancouver.

Kevin had fallen asleep almost immediately after they boarded. Erin sat in the middle seat watching Tory working on her colouring books. Tory looked completely focused, as if the only things in the universe were her crayons, her book, and the task of staying within the lines. She held her breath each time she coloured anywhere near a line. Then she would sit back, take a deep breath, and continue. Erin smiled as she recalled the sheer terror on Tory's face when she saw the reckless scribbling inside the colouring book of her playmate, Jeffrey, from down the street. At three and a half, Tory had already acquired a firm commitment to excellence. Erin wondered how much came from watching herself and Kevin, and how much was hardwired into her personality.

Earlier in the flight, Erin had thought about Carla, and how attractive and full of life she was. She was extremely charismatic. It was not hard to see how Brad had fallen for her. She was very much an artist, not just committed to her craft, but able to see the world in ways that most people could not, or perhaps would not. Within about an hour, Tory had expanded her dream of playing hockey at the Olympics to include a component of modern dance.

Although she felt ashamed for thinking it, Erin had felt envious of Carla and Tory's immediate gravitation towards her. It occurred to Erin now, that some of the unrest that she'd been feeling in months prior had to do with her and not Kevin. She wanted a craft. Something that was her own. A discipline through which to express herself.

The more she thought about it, the more disappointed she was that she had stopped thinking in those terms for herself. She was committed to Kevin and his goals as an athlete. She was committed to Tory and optimizing her development. But what commitment had she made to herself? In truth, her pregnancy with Tory had been taxing, requiring all of her faculties to get through it. But that seemed to offer little consolation three years after the fact.

She had about a year and a half left in her degree from UBC. She had always had a keen interest in sport nutrition, thinking she might like to have her own consulting business one day. But that just became another one of the things she did for Kevin.

As she reflected on her lost aspirations, she marveled at how easily they had vanished from her consciousness. How they had been overshadowed by Kevin's goals. But whose fault was that? Kevin had never discouraged her from continuing to pursue her interests. It occurred to her that he had even suggested she might pick up where she had left off.

Oh, Erin, quit looking for reasons to be depressed, she instructed herself when she realized what she was doing. *Quit crying over lost time. Decide what you want to do and do it!* Meeting Carla was at once uplifting and depressing. She had such energy and passion for her dancing. It could be inspiring if Erin didn't feel like she was at such a standstill. She sighed and let her mind wander to other things. At least her marriage seemed to be taking an upswing. She could be thankful for that. And Tory . . . , well she could enjoy that miracle every single day.

Tory had stopped colouring and sat in her seat uncomfortably. She seemed to be concealing something that was bothering her. She finally looked up at her mother, with a look of distress, and revealed the problem, "Mommy, my ears." As she got it out she began to cry, very quietly, not wanting to cause a fuss. Tory fought her tears the same way that Erin did. Erin wondered if it was learned.

She took a hard candy from her purse and handed it to Tory. "Have one of these, honey. It will help. And try yawning to clear your ears. Once we land you'll feel better, and it's not much longer." Tory nodded, trying to keep her bottom lip from protruding. It was a courageous effort, but a losing battle. Eventually she buried her face in her mother's side, and sobbed silently.

Kevin woke with a jolt of turbulence, squinting while his eyes adjusted. "What's wrong?" he asked, looking at Tory.

"It's her ears again. She'll be okay." Erin insisted, as she ran her fingers through Tory's hair to distract her from the pain.

"How about you?" Kevin asked, noticing the remnants of sadness on Erin's face.

"Oh . . . just tired, I think," she replied, mustering a half smile.

As promised, Tory felt much better once they had landed. Her energy returned, which seemed to help Erin to follow suit. They shuttled to the Park n' Ride and piled into the Cherokee.

"I should probably drop you guys off at home and head for the rink," Kevin suggested. "It's only seven thirty. I should be able to get over there in time to catch most of the second."

Erin nodded, "I completely forgot there was a game tonight."

"Not me," Kevin responded, "My conscience is still working overtime for my suspension. Man, I hope the boys can get it done tonight. We don't need a three game skid going into the playoffs. Oh, hey, it should be on the radio somewhere, right?" Erin shrugged.

Kevin searched the stations until he found the game. He turned the volume up, not wanting to miss anything. Erin assumed they were done talking for a while. The announcer boomed over the car speakers, "Well, the Vancouver fans have got to be pleased with what they've seen so far tonight. Goals by Krohn, Koshenko, and Kopp have given the Canucks a 3-0 lead with under seven minutes to play in the first."

The colour man continued, "That's right, Grant, and you could feel a buzz in the building when they announced Koshenko's 48th goal. I'm sure people are wondering if he might hit 50 tonight. It looked like he might have gotten a piece of that Kopp shot, but apparently it went straight in for Kopp's 15th. It's also worth noting that Kopp is sitting at 48 points. He and Vlad Koshenko see a lot of ice together. The way they're playing, they may hit 50 goals and 50 points together."

Kevin looked over at Erin, "Ah, that would be beauty."

Erin looked back, smiling, but with a look of amazement, "Well, that was a quick attitude shift."

Kevin looked a little embarrassed, and tried to explain, "Well, it's just that . . . I mean, I think I was kind of . . ."

Erin let him off the hook, "You don't have to explain. I mean, I think it's great. It's just surprising, that's all." She patted his thigh then rubbed it reassuringly. "You'd better hustle over there to see how it pans out."

Kevin smiled, relieved that he wasn't forced to articulate his bad attitude from before. He also seemed more relaxed from the moment he heard the score. It had been in the back of his mind that the blame for a losing streak might fall on his shoulders.

As the play-by-play resumed, Kevin noticed that Lars Soederberg was playing on the first line in stead of Conrad Soles. He wondered if Rick might have made that suggestion to Boucher. His advice seemed to carry a lot of weight with the coaching staff. In any case, Vlad seemed to be back in a rhythm.

When they arrived at the house, Kevin carried the heavy bags in, kissed both girls goodbye, and ran back to the car to head for GM Place. Erin found it refreshing to see him care so much about a game that he wasn't playing in. When he'd missed games for injuries before, he seemed to be indifferent about their outcomes. Something major had changed in the way Kevin saw the game. She assumed that it had to do with his talks with Cormie, but was less concerned with *why* it had happened, than simply being happy that it had.

While Kevin was driving to the rink, the second period began. It sounded as though his team was dominating most aspects of the game, again putting Kevin's mind at case.

"Koshenko picking up speed in the neutral zone. He slaps it into the Anaheim zone. Mason is unable to handle the puck and heads back to the net. Collette fishes it out of the corner and, Oooo! He's hit hard against the boards by Morrison, freeing the puck for Soederberg. Soederberg drives to the net, tries to jam it in the side. They're banging away, Mason sprawling, can't get the handle, scooooores!!!"

"Yes!" Kevin yelled, pumping his fist.

"I believe it was Koshenko who finally jammed it past Mason. He was hammered from behind, but appears to be okay. Yes, it's Koshenko, his 49th, assisted by Soederberg."

"Morrison won't get an assist, but it was his hit on Collette that made the play. And Grant, we've still got the better part of two periods to play, and the crowd senses that they're going to see Koshenko get his 50th tonight."

"Ata boy, Mo! Way to make it happen!" Kevin praised his linemate as he sat at a light.

Kevin watched Koshenko get his 50th from up in the press box. With five minutes left in the third period, Kyle Kopp caught Vladimir in full stride breaking up the middle. He watched with admiration as Koshenko waited patiently, then drove the puck between the pads of the goalie. He felt a faint prick of envy when the crowd stood to honour the achievement. The remnants of old feelings that had faded considerably. A week earlier, it would have felt like a knife through his heart.

At the horn, Kevin hurried down to the dressing room to share in celebrating the 6-1 victory. Rick was herding the last few players into the room before the media people could start interviewing. He directed Koshenko into the room gently, explaining to the reporters as he did, "Just a couple minutes, guys, then he's all yours."

The room quieted as Rick shut the door behind him. "Great game fellas, but I just want to say something quick before you take off. This was the momentum boost we needed going in, but let's not waste it by getting shit-faced tonight. Enjoy it. Go have a few if you like, but we've got St. Louis *in* St. Louis on Wednesday. That's four sleeps. So let's take good care of ourselves. Some guys are banged up. Pax said he'll be in tomorrow, so put him to work." Trainer, Tony Paxton, nodded his head from his spot in the corner. Rick finally gave in to the grin that he'd been concealing, then quietly closed his speech, "It's playoff time, boys."

The room erupted, led by Billy's familiar sentiments, "Fuckin' rights, boys! Fuckin' bring it on!"

25

GM Place. Eleven days later.

Kevin got out of his Cherokee and walked towards the players' entrance. He was the first player to arrive at the rink. Tonight he would try to turn the fortunes of his team. The first three games of the playoffs replayed in his head, like a series of bad dreams.

Game one in St. Louis had been a complete disaster. Rookie goaltender Stephane Oullett had gotten the nod. Behind closed doors, Jamie Harris had convinced Boucher to give him the start. He argued that it would take something special to steal a win in St. Louis. While Jack Simmons was a solid veteran back-up, he was not healthy, and would probably play even with opposing starting goaltenders at best. Oullett had shown signs of brilliance in the minors. Maybe this was his time. Against his instincts, Boucher agreed. His fears were realized. Oullett let in a weak goal a minute and a half in and never really regained his confidence.

The St. Louis game plan was simple; smother Vladimir Koshenko. The twin towers of the St. Louis defense stepped onto the ice every time he did. They bounced him around like a pinball for three hours. To his credit, Vladimir took the punishment and kept coming, scoring the only Vancouver goal on the power play.

Billy Morrison was ejected after a third fighting major, repeatedly coming to the aid of his superstar linemate. Even Rick lost his cool towards the end of the game, objecting to the punishment that Koshenko had endured. Thousands of miles away, Kevin watched on T.V., paralyzed by frustration, furious at the St. Louis players, ashamed about his absence. 5-1 was the final.

Game two hadn't gone much better. With Jack Simmons in goal, the Canucks were downed 7-3. Koshenko was held to one assist on a goal by Morrison. The second line showed some offensive spark with goals from Olsen and Krohn, but didn't fair as well in the defensive zone, giving up four goals. All-star defenseman, Kyle Kopp, left the game midway through the third with a concussion. He was hit from behind, resulting in a five-minute power play that his team failed to score on. Again, Kevin had to watch helplessly from his couch. Erin's attempts to comfort him had no effect. Even some colouring with Tory during the first intermission failed to calm his nerves.

Game three was the most frustrating to watch. Despite the 1-0 final score, the game was again dominated by the Blues. From the press box, Kevin watched his team get outshot 36-11. A dismal offensive outing for the team in front of a home crowd. If there was a silver lining, it was the outstanding play of Stephane Oullett, who rebounded brilliantly from the game one beating. But the team was still without Kopp, and their go-to scorer looked weary, as if the St. Louis pounding had finally taken its toll.

But as Kevin walked through the corridor, he convinced himself that tonight would be different. Kopp was back in the line-up. Oullett was confident and had shown the team that he could give them a chance. And the top line of himself, Vladimir, and Billy would be reunited. Together, they had accounted for over half of the Vancouver goals during the regular season.

Kevin walked to the ice surface and sat down at the home bench. He began visualizing the things that he wanted to make happen on the ice. Finishing every one of his checks. Driving hard to the St. Louis net, into it if necessary. Helping out in the defensive zone. Getting the puck on net, and following it. Creating space for Koshenko with his speed.

An unexpected smile came over his face as he prepared for the game. Suddenly the challenge of being down 3-0 in the series excited him. He felt like he was in a Rocky movie. The image of overcoming these odds was thrilling. He was ready to play. He hoped his teammates felt the same way.

Minutes before the game, the dressing room was quiet but relaxed. The tension that had filled the room for the three previous games had passed. It had a 'nothing-to-lose' feel about it.

Kevin glanced sideways at Billy, whose head bobbed up and down to music so heavy that his teammates wouldn't let him put it in the stereo. Kevin tapped Billy on the shins with his stick and winked at him when he looked over. Billy's eye's widened and tongue protruded, partly poking fun at his own choice of music, but partly unable to conceal his excitement.

Kevin's legs felt shaky under him as he lined up to walk out. He hadn't played at home in three weeks. But he knew the jitters would disappear after his first shift. Rick slapped the front of his pants sharply with his stick and nodded at him as he walked to the front of the line. The captain's routine was to touch each player on his way to the front, looking each of them in the eyes, smiling at the players who looked a little too tense to loosen them up.

Kyle Kopp's voice echoed through the corridor, reassuring his teammates that he was ready, "Let's go now, eh, boys! This our barn now! Let's take it to 'em!"

Billy barked his approval bouncing as he spoke, "Ata way Kopper, crank it up now, baby! Woo!"

Kevin stood quietly, rolling his shoulders to shrug off his goose bumps. The feeling of camaraderie was almost overwhelming. Remarkably, the atmosphere was not that of a team who had been beaten soundly in three straight contests. It was electric. He could feel hope resonating through the line, from Oullett at the front with Rick, back to defensive forward, Corey Lynch, who insisted on being the last one out of the room.

Rick's line started against the top line of the Blues. The crowd roared as Rick rode the Blues' top scorer, Janne Aalto into the boards, pushing him off the puck. The St. Louis players seemed surprised at the intensity that the Canucks came out with, although Kevin assumed that they would have been told to expect it. Teams with nothing to lose can play with a lot of energy.

"Shenk's line go!" Boucher yelled as Soederberg chipped the puck into the St. Louis zone. The Blues advanced the puck, gaining the center line and shooting it in. The puck took a funny bounce back out in front of the Canuck's net. The winger slapped the puck towards the net. It was redirected towards the corner by a stick, with Oullett moving the other way across the crease. In desperation, he flailed at it with his stick. The puck went off the edge of his stick, off the crossbar, and was batted away by Canuck defenseman, Petr Sopel.

Back the other way, Koshenko led the rush. He flipped a pass neatly over a defender's stick to Kevin. Kevin let a low shot go, but the goalie got a pad on it and covered up. On the other wing, Billy had a St. Louis defender draped over him as he sped to the net. Both players barreled into the goalie, knocking him back into the net. All of the players around the net had their sticks up in the skirmish that followed. Kevin was right in the middle. Billy fought his way out from under the pile, facewashing a Blues' defender with his glove as he glided backwards. Kevin's heart nearly pounded out of his chest, captured by the intensity of the moment, eager to back up his teammates. The building was buzzing, excited by the raw energy that the Canucks had brought to the ice for this game.

The crowd voiced their disapproval with the penalties assessed. Two Blues players went off for roughing, along with Kevin and Billy. But Billy picked up the extra minor for goaltender interference, giving the Blues their first power play. In spite of his seat in the penalty box, Kevin felt great, still swimming in adrenaline. "It's alright, Mo. We're setting the pace, buddy. This is gonna be a war." Billy's head nodded quickly. He sat at the edge of the bench, too fired up to respond verbally.

The Blues controlled the puck in the Canuck zone, moving the puck around crisply. Rick dropped to the ice, to block a shot from the blueline. The puck took a hard bounce off of his shin pad. Corey Lynch, the other forward on the penalty kill knocked the defenseman's stick away from his body to avoid being hooked, and raced to the loose puck. He hustled down the wing with two St. Louis defenders in pursuit, letting a slapshot go from a bad angle. He turned in to the net slapping at his own rebound. Kyle Kopp followed him in, jamming the puck past the St. Louis goalie.

Kevin barely saw the red light go on, signaling the goal, before he was tackled onto the bench by Billy. The crowd was on its feet, applauding the team's first lead in the series.

In the half period that followed, St. Louis reasserted themselves as the favourite, peppering the Canucks' rookie goaltender with shots. However, despite the onslaught, Oullett managed to keep the Blues off the scoreboard. And the sometimes shaky Canucks' defensive corps stood up to the powerful St. Louis forwards, preventing second and third opportunities on the rebound.

Finally, Kevin produced another spark for the Canucks. Taking a pass from Koshenko, he sped into the Blues' zone, squeezing between a Blues' defenseman and the boards. Too far out to cut in to the net, he cut behind the net and around the other side. As he circled in front of the Blues' net, two Blues' defenders converged on him. But, waiting patiently, he snapped the puck sharply over the left shoulder of the goalie, before being knocked heavily to the ice by the force of both defenders.

From his back, Kevin saw the blur of lights and the hazy forms of two faces above him. Kevin tried to blink away the cobwebs, and was finally able to make out the faces of Billy and Vladimir above him. Kevin climbed slowly to his feet, his vision and balance quickly returning to normal. 2-0.

On the bench, trainer, Tony Paxton, scurried in behind Kevin, "Talk to me, Wilk. You alright?"

Kevin nodded as he swallowed a mouthful of Powerade, "Yeah, I'm good, Pax. Just got my bell rung a little." Kevin looked back over his shoulder, smiling, "Thanks though, little buddy."

Paxton snickered, "Hey, I'm here for ya."

In the second period, the Blues showed how they led the regular season so convincingly. They tied the game up, scoring two goals, forty seconds apart, including a twenty-foot laser by Janne Aalto that even the Vancouver crowd had to admire.

During the second intermission, the Canuck locker room was buzzing with activity. Jamie Harris was huddled up with the defensemen, discussing strategic adjustments to contain the top St. Louis forwards. Players compared mental notes across the room. Many players attempted to pump up Stephane Oullett's confidence, going into the final period.

Kevin sat back and watched, recognizing a feeling he'd seen little evidence of in his years with this team. Each and every player believed that they would win. He could see it in their eyes. He heard it in their voices.

He felt it himself, in his chest and his shoulders. He felt a tingle down his spine and glanced down at his forearms. He had goose bumps. *Man, this is fun,* he thought to himself. Billy looked at him, a smile coming over his face. They touched fists and enjoyed the moment, with no words required to verify what they were both feeling.

The third period was evenly fought, neither team giving up many scoring chances. The Blues did a good job of containing the Canucks' first line, but Kevin, Billy, and Vlad seemed to gain energy as the period went on, continuously testing the Blues' defenders.

Eventually, they gained control of the puck in the St. Louis zone. Vladimir dug it out of the feet of a Blues' defenseman that Billy had tied up behind the net. He spun out of the corner, narrowly escaping a check, driving to the front of the net. When two defenders rushed towards him, he feathered a pass between the legs of one defender, over to Kevin beside the net. Kevin one-timed the shot heavily into the Blues net. He raised his stick in the air to celebrate, then pointed at Vladimir to credit him for the pass. The two players came together and hugged, before being mauled by Billy who knocked all three to the ice. 3-2.

Oullet continued to impress in the Canucks' net, determined to protect the lead. But as the third period neared completion, he faced fewer and fewer shots, as his team gained confidence in shutting down the St. Louis rush.

Finally, the Canucks got the back-breaker. With the Blues goalie pulled, Kopp slapped the puck around the boards and it was mishandled at the blueline, bouncing off a St. Louis glove, and into the neutral zone. Rick won the race to the loose puck, chipping it ahead to Soederberg, who directed the puck carefully into the empty net. 4-2. The Vancouver crowd applauded the effort for the remaining minute of play. The Vancouver players converged on Stephane Oullett to celebrate the win.

Kevin was pulled aside after his first star announcement for a T.V. interview.

"Congrats on a big win, Kevin. How big is this for your hockey club?"

"Oh, it's huge. We know now that we can beat these guys. We just have to go out in game five with the same jump."

"It looked like a different team out there with you in the line-up. What do you feel that you bring to the team that may have been lacking in the first three games?"

Kevin's eyes narrowed slightly, uncomfortable with the notion that he'd been the only difference. "Well, I think two things were huge. Steph had another unbelievable game in net, and that first goal by Kopper gave us a real boost. Even when they came back and tied it, it felt like they were chasing us tonight, instead of the other way around."

The reporter continued to fish, "It didn't hurt that you potted a couple either."

Kevin shrugged, "I think there was a bit of a mix-up on that first one, so I was able to move right in and shoot. And for my second goal, I had the best seat in the house for the Vlad Koshenko show. That set-up was picture perfect."

"Thanks, Kevin. Good luck in St. Louis."

"Thanks, Scott."

As Kevin walked into the locker room, he remembered little from his interview. He didn't give it much thought. He had just described what he saw, rather than searching for the right words. It felt easy, rather than scripted. His whole life was starting to feel that way.

26

A small apartment in Saskatoon.

Brad and Carla were curled up on a couch, watching T.V. On the screen, a reply of Kevin's first goal played in slow motion.

Brad shook his head as he smiled, "Man, I'd forgotten how good he was. He really was made for this game."

Carla nestled into Brad's chest and responded, "Just like his little brother."

Brad shook his head, sitting up slightly. "No, it's a totally different game at that level. Everyone out there is so good."

Carla sat up straight, sitting cross-legged, and turned to face Brad squarely. "You've been thinking a lot about Columbus, haven't you?" Brad nodded, staring off at the wall. "Brad, I don't understand why you're so uneasy about this. You love playing. You didn't get into med school this time around, but you will. So go and give it a shot. What have you got to lose?"

"But shouldn't I just start grad school, get some leverage for my application next year?" Brad asked, seeking guidance.

Carla took both of Brad's hands in hers, pulled him forward, and kissed him on the forehead. "There'll be time for that. Look, if I thought your heart was pulling you to med school at this point in your life, I'd say 'forget hockey, focus on school'. But I've seen how happy you are on the ice. And I think you feel the same way that I feel when I dance. You feel free." Brad smiled, conceding to Carla's intuition. Carla continued, "I also saw the look in your eyes after that play-off loss, when you thought you'd played your last game. It's not time yet, Brad." She smiled and touched his nose, laughing gently, "Surely you don't need me to tell you that."

Brad looked away, absorbing Carla's comments, then took on a far away expression. "It's not the hockey I'm worried about, Car. It's the business. It's ugly. They squeeze the fun out of the game. No one gives a shit about you there."

Carla nodded politely, waiting to speak. "What do you love about the game?" Brad looked puzzled by the question. Carla prompted him again, "Just answer. What do you love about the game?"

Brad took a deep breath and went along. "I love the speed, the rush of the pace. I love the contact." Brad's shoulders relaxed as he spoke, "I love the feel of a team that comes together, like you'd take a bullet for anyone on it. I love lining up and looking across at the other team, wondering who wants it more. I just . . . I just love to play. You know, just playing. Not worrying about what it means to win or lose, just feeling the game."

Carla smiled and nodded along as Brad spoke. "Then make the game about those things when you go. Make it what you want it to be. No one can ruin it for you if you don't let them."

Brad nodded, looking straight ahead. His mouth opened and he took a short breath in, as if he were about to speak. Then he let it out heavily and paused. Carla waited quietly. She knew he had more to say.

"Maybe I'm a little scared about not making it. I mean, what if I go and give it my best shot and that's not good enough. So many people would think they were right about me all along. I mean, there are a lot of people that would like to see me fail after the way I walked away from junior."

Carla's brow wrinkled, looking annoyed at what she was hearing, "What do we care of those people? They're nothing to us. If you don't make it, you'll come back to the hotel with me, we'll make love until the morning, and then we'll talk about what's next over breakfast." She pulled him close by the shoulders and continued quietly, "We're not going to let the past interfere with our dreams. Especially the people that want to see us fail. Oh Brad, if all you could do is play hockey, I could understand this fear, but you're so much more than that. You're a beautiful, beautiful man. You're smart, you're funny, you're creative. You're passionate, you're gentle, you care about people. You can't lose any of that if you don't make a hockey team. Don't go to prove yourself. Go because when you're out there you can experience some of the magic that makes you you. Go because of the way you feel when you play, all the things you described to me."

Brad pulled his fiance in to hug her. They rocked side to side, squeezing tightly. Brad kissed her ear and whispered into it, "God I love you, Car. Somehow, you know how to melt away all my crap."

Carla smiled and pulled back to see Brad's face, her eyes squinting from her smile, "It's easy. I just love it away, Aranyom." Brad smiled shyly at the Hungarian pet name that she had for him. It meant 'my golden', which was how he always felt when he was with her.

27

Kevin lay face down on the bed with his shirt off. Erin sat on his back, massaging it, raising her arms occasionally to shake her sleeves back up to keep from touching them with her oily hands.

As she massaged, Erin quizzed Kevin. "Brown-eyed Girl."

"Van Morrison."

"Okay, too easy. Um . . . Raise a Little Hell."

"Trooper."

"Um . . . I Go Blind."

"54-40."

"Ha! Wrong. It's Hootie and the Blowfish." Erin sat up and clapped.

"Hootie redid it. It was 54-40's song." Kevin laughed awkwardly with Erin on his back. "They're a Vancouver band, you loser."

Erin laughed along, "Well I don't know! I just knew the Hootie one!"

Kevin prompted her to continue, "Come on 'Rock Jeopardy Queen', bring it on!"

Erin squinted, cocking her head as she searched for a stumper. "Alright hot shot, ummmm . . . Sister Golden Hair."

Kevin held his breath in a slight panic, searching his memory, "Oh crap! Oh, I know this."

"Five seconds," Erin pressured.

"Oh, come on, it's . . ."

"Time's up. Ha! It's America, Rock Jeopardy King!" Erin bobbed her head, mocking playfully. "My turn."

Erin climbed off and lay down on her stomach, pulling her shirt up to expose her back. Kevin climbed onto her gently and began to massage her. "Okay, football or baseball?"

"Um, football."

Kevin smirked, "Okay Wilk, but this is where I stumped you last time."

"I'm ready this time. This is gonna be a long massage." Erin giggled as she taunted.

"New England."

"Um . . . Patriots?"

"Yep. Almost had you right off the bat. Okay, San Francisco."

"Forty-Niners. A little lower please, massage boy."

Both laughed at Erin's trash-talking. She could never quite pull it off without cracking up. They continued the trivia massage game until Erin had listed most of the teams in the NFL, finally stumped by the Tennessee Titans. Kevin got up and walked to the ensuite to wash the oil off of his hands.

He slowed near the doorway and felt for the frame to steady himself.

"Kev, you okay?" Erin asked looking increasingly concerned.

Kevin appeared to snap out of it. "Yeah. Just a little dizzy there for a second. Must have stood up too fast." He continued into the bathroom to wash up. Erin's concern continued to show in her expression.

She leaned into the bathroom, "You're sure you're okay?"

"Yeah. I'm sure. It's okay. I'm probably good and tired too."

"Alright, if you're sure," Erin replied, not quite looking convinced.

They got ready and slipped into bed, neither of them quite wanting their evening to end, with Kevin leaving for St. Louis the next day.

"Goodnight, sweetie." Kevin said, kissing Erin on the lips.

"Okay, I guess we'd better go to sleep," Erin said reluctantly. She lay awake watching her husband sleep, wondering if she'd seen another sign of concussion, or if it really had been nothing. This wasn't the first dizzy spell she'd witnessed this season. She finally convinced herself that he was okay and drifted off to sleep.

Kevin woke up early and took Tory to the park nearby. They'd negotiated some pushes on the swing and the merry-go-round before his departure. She had worked breakfast at McDonald's into the deal, but Erin overturned the agreement, not wanting Kevin to be tempted to eat poorly during the play-offs.

Kevin threw his bags in the Cherokee and jogged back to the door where his wife and daughter waited. To Erin, his face seemed to shine with excitement.

"You're having a lot of fun, aren't you?" Erin asked, knowing the answer.

"I honestly can't remember the last time the game was so fun. I don't know if it's just the play-offs or what," Kevin replied, not trying too hard to figure it out.

"Probably a combination of things," Erin speculated, resisting the temptation to get too philosophical right before his departure. "Talk to you tonight?"

"Yep. You can talk me down so I'll sleep well."

Erin smiled, happy that Kevin saw her as a partner in his pursuit. Kevin bent down on one knee to kiss Tory goodbye. "Be good, L. Dub. I'll see you in a few days."

Tory wrapped her arms around her father's neck, almost choking him, "Bye, Daddy! Good luck in the play-office."

Kevin and Erin looked at each other and giggled, mutually deciding Tory's mistake was too cute to correct just yet. Kevin stood up and pulled Erin in for a hug, kissing her on the lips. "Love you sweetie. Talk to you later."

Erin squeezed him once more, not quite satisfied with the first one. "Love you too. Go get 'em."

The two girls waved as the jeep pulled away, Kevin's hand reaching across the passenger seat to wave back.

28

Game 5. Kiel Center, St. Louis.

Kevin, Billy, and Vlad glided to center for the opening face-off. The arena was sold out and the crowd was excited and noisy. The same air of confidence had been present in the Canuck locker room, even though they were on the road and still on the ropes at 3-1 in the series.

It was a fire-cracker first period, with both teams playing the body ferociously. Kevin and Billy led the charge, banging away at the St. Louis defense every chance they got. Shots were few, legitimate scoring opportunities even fewer. Shift after shift, Kevin and Billy came back to the bench and touched gloves with anyone on the bench that could reach them.

Late in the first period, Kevin dumped the puck into the St. Louis zone along the boards. The Blues' fifth defenseman, Marty Stokes, hustled behind the net to play the puck. With Morrison coming towards him with a head of steam, Stokes hurried a pass up the middle to a Blues' forward. Vladimir stepped in front to intercept the pass and snapped the puck sharply through the legs of the St. Louis goaltender. It happened so quickly, it took the Vancouver players a moment to realize what had happened. The crowd was silent as the Canuck players converged on Koshenko to celebrate. It was still 1-0 Vancouver at the end of the first.

In the locker room, you could feel the momentum that the Canucks had gained. The room was composed but a buzz of anticipation was evident as they made minor adjustments for the second. Rick seemed to temper the excitement, keeping it from getting too high. Kevin watched with admiration as Rick discussed defensive zone play calmly with Boucher, as if it were a practice.

In the second period, the powerful offense of the Blues started to click, but the Canucks conceded nothing, matching the Blues shot for shot. The Canuck second line had the best chances but failed to capitalize, as Blues' tender, Darcy Billings, had recovered from the first goal, and looked very sharp in the second.

With two minutes to play in the second, Blues defenseman, Carson Gill, was passing the puck up ice when he was bumped by Corey Lynch. In one motion, Lynch checked Gill lightly and turned quickly to skate back to pursue the play. As he turned, his stick came around and clipped Gill under the eye, cutting him. Gill glided to the bench, holding his eye and the play was stopped. Although the high stick was accidental, the cut was a bad one, and Lynch was assessed a five minute major penalty and a game misconduct, putting him out for the remainder of the game.

The Canucks now had two problems. They would have to try to kill off a five minute power play against the highest scoring team in the NHL. They would also have to finish the game without one of their strongest defensive players. But if there was a bright side, it was the fact that they could split the penalty kill in two, with two minutes left in the second and the other three to start the third.

They got off to a shaky start. Right off the face-off, a shot from the blueline was tipped past Oullett by Blues' sniper, Janne Aalto, with Kyle

Kopp draped all over him. 1-1. The crowd erupted. The noise was almost deafening and the Canuck players sat on the bench subdued by the cheers. They tried to ignore the fans shaking the plexi-glass behind them while contending with the sick feeling in their stomachs from their lead being erased.

With thirty seconds to play in the period, the Blues again controlled the puck in the Vancouver zone. Billy got his stick on a pass between the two defenseman, tipping it into the neutral zone. He beat both defensemen to the puck and raced towards the St. Louis net. Fighting off the two defenders hooking him from behind, Billy was able to flip the puck up when Billings, the goalie, tried to poke it away, gambling that the defenders had Morrison tied up sufficiently. The puck glanced off of Billings' shoulder and trickled into the net, followed by Billings, Morrison, and the two Blues' defenders. 2-1 Vancouver.

The resolve of the Canuck players seemed to strengthen as the game progressed. They easily killed off the remaining three minutes of the Blues' powerplay in the third, then proceeded to dominate play at even strength. Again and again, Vancouver's top line tested Billings, but he continued to keep the puck out. Vlad and Kevin registered four shots each in the third but Billings was equal to the test.

With seven minutes to play, the Canucks went into a neutral zone trap, making it almost impossible for the St. Louis forwards to get the puck into the Vancouver zone. They played as a single synchronous unit, executing their defensive roles to near perfection.

With a little over a minute to play, St. Louis pulled their goalie, sending out the extra man. They managed to get into the Canuck zone and earn a face-off with twenty-three seconds to play. Boucher sent out Rick, Billy, and Lars Soederberg, the three forwards that he felt were the strongest defensively that were still in the game. Rick won the face-off back to Kopp who tried to flip it out of the zone, but the rangy Carson Gill, who had returned to the game all stitched up, jumped up and knocked it down. With Billy pressuring him, Gill flipped a weak wrist shot at the net. The puck fluttered through the traffic in front of the net, over Oullett's shoulder. He never even saw it. The crowd exploded once again while the Canuck players shook their heads collectively in disbelief. Eleven seconds away from forcing a sixth game, the Canucks saw their lead fall on a fluke. 2-2.

In the locker room, before the overtime, Rick pleaded with his team to bounce back. "It's just shitty luck, fellas. But we've got to let it go. We're in a great spot. Next goal wins in their barn, and we've been getting the better chances. Let's crank it up now!"

Kevin added, "Hell yeah, boys. We're takin' it to 'em out there! Great work on the boards, tough 'D'. Steph's razor sharp in the pipes. This thing's ours. Let's just go out and get it."

Gradually, faces came up and heads nodded. They were ready for their next challenge. Overtime.

Both teams came out slugging with great chances at both ends. But Billings and Oullett continued to shine in goal. As both teams showed signs of fatigue from the blistering pace that had been set in the first two periods, there were more and more good chances to score.

Finally, the Canucks controlled the puck in the Blues' zone and passed the puck back to Kopp at the blueline. With Conrad Soles blocking Billings' vision in front of the net, Kopp let a low, hard shot go on net. The puck ricocheted off of a defender's shin pad who was wrestling for position with Soles. The puck hit the post and bounced out. Soles lunged to swing at the puck, but Matteus Krohn had already sped in from the wing and tapped it in.

The Canucks' bench emptied, and players rushed to jump on the pile with Krohn at the bottom. Darcy Billings was furious, pursuing the referee to protest the goal. He stopped his protest when he realized that the official was waving it off. The Canuck players argued vehemently, but the replay on the scoreboard revealed that Soles did in fact bump Billings when he went for the puck. So their protests turned to resignation, seeing that the call was the only one the referee could have made.

The referee called Rick and the Blues captain to the penalty box to explain the ruling. The Vancouver bench was further deflated when they saw the always-composed Rick Olsen turn away from the official rolling his eyes and shaking his head. He glided slowly over to the Vancouver bench to fill Boucher in on the call. "He said Solesy interfered with Billings, so he gets two for goaltender interference".

Boucher couldn't hide his disappointment, "Ah, for Christ sake!" He paused and refocused, "Alright, Olse, Mo, start us off. Let's kill this thing off."

The Blues shot the puck into the Canuck zone and were able to regain possession. They moved the puck around crisply until Gill let a heavy shot go from the point. Rick was able to block it, but it came straight back to Gill who restarted the Blues passing around the zone. Billy and Rick were moving well with the puck, making it difficult to set up a shot that would get through. Gill finally caught Billy sneaking out a little too far and whistled a crisp pass directly to Russ McNair, the standout rookie, who one-timed the puck under Oullett's glove hand. This time there was no protest. The Blues had won the game and eliminated the Canucks in five games.

The Canucks' room was solemn after the game. Players got out of their gear slowly, occasionally shaking hands or patting backs to console or commend the effort. Kevin sat with only his shoulder pads and helmet off, and glanced over at Rick.

"What?" Rick asked inquisitively.

"Hmm?" Kevin replied.

"You're thinking something. I want to know what it is," Rick continued impatiently.

"Well, actually, I was just thinking . . . of course I'm choked about losing and everything, but . . ." Kevin paused.

"But what?" Rick insisted.

"That was so much fun." Kevin finished his thought, almost apologetically.

Rick looked a little confused then sat back and pondered what his young friend had said. Finally, a faint smile came over his face, and he looked back at Kevin and nodded.

29

Although everyone was down from the loss, being with the team felt good to Kevin. Everyone had put everything they had into this game. So they all needed to feel badly about the outcome for a little while. Although disappointment was the most obvious emotion that cut across the members of the team, another feeling was unmistakably present. Everyone felt like they belonged. Everyone felt a part of something bigger than themselves. As they got off the bus at the airport, Kevin didn't feel like he wanted to be anywhere else. For now, he was where he needed to be.

While they walked to the terminal, Kevin reflected on Boucher's post-game remarks. It was their first play-off appearance in five years. And in games four and five, they tested the mettle of the league's most dominant team. Boucher's words echoed in his mind. "Don't drive yourselves crazy wondering what might have happened if we'd won tonight. There's no point. Instead, take some satisfaction in the job. In the past two games, we got a taste of the future. The last two games showed us how we can play if we're willing to put ourselves on the line, if we're willing to go the distance. Take some time to feel bad about this loss if you need to, but when you're done, start dreaming about what's possible next season. I was proud to stand behind you guys this year. Thanks gentlemen."

Coach Boucher was a man of few words, but those that he chose to speak, he chose carefully. His speech was healing for the players. As was typical in a game this close, most of the players had already identified a missed opportunity that made the loss their fault. Boucher's words allowed the players to feel pride and disappointment simultaneously, something that many athletes never allow themselves to do.

As the players crowded together at the gate, Rick huddled them together for a quick reminder. "No D&S's on the plane, okay fellas?" (Rick's code for drunk and stupid), "If you're gonna booze, do it in Vancouver." Most of the players nodded. Those who didn't were too tired to even think about drinking heavily.

Kevin sat beside Rick on the plane. As they sat quietly, Rick's eyelids grew heavy and he started to drift off when he heard Kevin's voice beside him. "Sorry I've been such a dick lately, Olse." Rick's eyes opened fully and he turned towards Kevin. This seemed like an odd time to get into it, but it had to happen eventually.

"Actually, I've seen a pretty refreshing change lately, Kev." Rick replied, sitting up straight.

"Well, I guess I should say for most of this year." Kevin clarified. "But I want you to know that I'm gonna make things right." Rick was now wide awake, curious about where Kevin was leading to.

"How so?" He asked.

"Well, I've been trying to be a better team guy in the last little while. I think success was going to my head a little," Kevin explained. Rick thought to himself that success had gone to Kevin's head *a lot*, but saw this admission as a breakthrough nonetheless.

"I don't mean to be too blunt, but does all this have to do with Gord McCormack's death?" Rick asked, deciding to break the discussion wide open.

"That's a big part of it, I guess. Well, actually, no. It really has nothing to do with his death. It's really about what we talked about before he died. . . . I guess maybe his death kind of made what he had to say seem more urgent, if that makes any sense," Kevin said, clearly dissatisfied with his explanation.

Rick nodded reassuringly, "It makes sense."

"But I knew things were coming undone before I went to see him. I mean, things were falling to pieces with Erin, and I was obsessed with my stats and stuff. The blow-up in Dallas. Everything just felt wrong. I felt like *our* friendship was kind of fading away. It's like, all of a sudden, I didn't know who I'd become. I was just trapped in this insecure little world."

"With none of the people closest to you," Rick added.

"Exactly. So when I went to see Cormie, he saw through it all right away. He helped me to see what I was focused on. He helped me to see why it was a shitty focus. But he also reminded me that it's never too late to make things right. Now I'm having more fun at the rink. I don't really care about stats, and getting credit, and all that stuff. Things are great with Erin again."

"How about Tory?" Rick probed.

"Things are always great with Tory. She's been the one constant in my life. She's probably the one person that's kept me from losing it altogether," Kevin speculated while Rick nodded along, smiling. "She wished me good luck in the 'play-office' before I left" Kevin said laughing.

Rick's smile turned to laughter, "She's a cutie alright."

Kevin returned to his line of thought. "It's like I've discovered how to live again. But I'm stuck on one point." Rick's smile faded as he listened intently. Kevin lowered his voice and looked down at the empty seat between them, not feeling like he could look at his friend as he continued. "He insisted that I tell Erin that I haven't been faithful . . . you knew that, right?"

Rick nodded, "Yeah . . . I knew. So what are you stuck on?"

Kevin looked up at Rick, his eyes pleading for understanding. "It would just kill her, Olse. And I don't think she could ever forgive me for that. That's just too much to ask. And lately it's like I've fallen in love with her all over again. So the thought of losing her just rips me to shreds." Kevin took a deep breath and rubbed his eyes then looked over at Rick, "How could I ever tell her?"

Rick let out a heavy sigh, then attempted to smile reassuringly. All he could manage was a slight curl on one side of his mouth. "You're right, Kev. It is too much to ask. But maybe she *can* forgive you. Maybe her love for you and for Tory and everything you've committed to together will give her the strength to stay, and in time forgive, . . . and eventually, maybe to trust you again."

Kevin hung his head in exasperation, "That sounds like a long road."

Rick nodded, "It is."

Kevin looked up, finally wondering why Rick seemed to speak so surely about the topic. "Have you . . . ?" Kevin asked, not needing to finish his sentence.

"Yeah. We went through this after Kate's miscarriage. It was a pretty tough couple of years for both of us," Rick said, staring at the seat in front of him. Then he turned to Kevin again, "But we got through it. I don't really want to go into the particulars, but Kev, you've got to believe me when I tell you . . . not telling her . . . it's not an option. You think it's tearing you apart now? Wait a while. The more you realize how much you love her, the worse you're gonna feel about yourself. And by the time it all comes out, you'll be too weak to hold it together."

Kevin stared blankly past Rick into the darkness out the window. He could not refute Rick's advice, as badly as he wished he could. He knew it was right. He felt it in his soul. But he was afraid. Afraid that all that had come together for him could suddenly fall apart.

"And what if she leaves . . . and takes Tory? What if that's it?" Kevin asked, the hope leaving his voice.

"Then at least you gave her the freedom to choose, based on the truth. And you're finished living a lie. It's the right thing, Kev. I didn't say it was the easy thing. But I'll do everything I can to help. So will Kate. You won't be alone if that's what you choose to do."

Rick looked at Kevin, hoping for some sort of reply, seeing none. Finally, when he could no longer stand the silence, he tried to offer some consolation. "For what it's worth, I'm really impressed that you've figured so much of this stuff out. I kept wanting to bring it up, but I knew it would just come across as a lecture and probably wouldn't do much good." Still no response. "Ah, come on, Kev. Things have a funny way of working out for the best. Do what you know is right, and at the end of the day, at least you can answer to yourself."

Kevin stared ahead blankly. Finally, his face took on a heavy expression, he swallowed, and nodded solemnly as he looked ahead. Rick patted him on the shoulder, confident that there wasn't much more that could be said.

When Kevin got home, he put his bags down to get out his key when the door opened. Erin looked out at him, obviously tired, but too excited to see her husband to sleep. Her smile had a hint of sympathy. She was used to consoling him after big losses.

Kevin stepped in with his bags, hurried to put them down, and hugged her, lifting her off her feet. "You're still up. I thought you'd be asleep."

Erin yawned, then her yawn turned to a big, tired smile, "I couldn't sleep. I wanted to see you. You guys were great tonight."

"Thanks. It was pretty exciting. I thought Krohnie'd put it away for us though," Kevin replied, remembering the finish.

"Yeah, that must have been pretty tough," Erin added, tilting her head slightly to convey her sympathy.

"Them's the breaks, I guess." Kevin pulled Erin in and hugged her again, "I missed you." He squeezed her even tighter this time.

Erin giggled a little, unsure what to think of Kevin's sentiment, after only a two-day absence. "I missed you too, honey." Erin hugged back, content just to enjoy the moment.

For a second, Kevin contemplated sitting her down and telling her the whole truth. But the mere thought of it exhausted him, knowing that the fallout would be more than he could bear when he was this tired. Erin saw the fatigue in his face and took him by the hand, "Bedtime, honey. And you can sleep in as late as you want tomorrow." She laughed and continued, "I'll try to keep Tory off of you until you're done sleeping."

Kevin smiled and dragged himself up the stairs, with Erin following. He got ready for bed and crawled under the covers, his body welcoming the feel of the mattress, like a dry throat welcomes water. Erin crawled in with him and cuddled up next to him. Kevin ran his fingers through her hair softly as they lay still. Erin fell asleep almost immediately, but Kevin lay awake, his eyes still open. He savoured the feel of her pressed against him. He breathed in her smell, over and over. He watched her side rise slightly with every breath, stricken by her delicate frame, by her innocence. Before finally being overcome with fatigue, he wondered if this was the last time that he would ever lay with her.

30

Erin woke to the sound of giggles downstairs. She blinked the fog from her eyes and tried to focus on the alarm clock. It was 7:30. She leaned across Kevin's side of the bed to listen. His spot on the bed was cool, suggesting that he'd been up for some time. Erin slipped on her housecoat and walked downstairs.

When she walked into the living room, she saw Tory and Kevin sitting cross-legged on the floor, each with a handful of cards. They would simultaneously put down a card, the higher card taking both, until finally they both put down cards of the same value. Both Tory's and Kevin's eyes widened and they looked across at each other, shouting in unison, "WAR!"

Tory giggled gleefully as they lay down three more cards each, in the winner take all show-down. Erin smiled and knelt down next to them to watch. They both looked up and smiled, acknowledging her, then returned their focus to the game. Tory bounced as she won the eight cards in the war.

"How many cards do you have left, Daddy?" Tory asked excitedly.

"Looks like about ten . . . but I'm coming back!" Kevin replied playfully.

Tory's eyes lit up as she took a deep breath, her determination growing, and she accelerated the pace of the game, sensing victory.

Erin walked into the kitchen to start a pot of tea, and discovered that one was already steeping and a cup was on the table. Also on the table were three bowls, two of them empty, and a third at Erin's spot, filled with freshly cut fruit. In the middle was a bag of granola and a container of yogurt, both with enough for one more helping. Erin sat down to eat the breakfast that had been left for her, turning her chair so that she could watch the conclusion of the card game.

When Tory won Kevin's last card, she stood up and leaned into Kevin, "Good game, Daddy," she said, congratulating him on his effort.

"Thanks, L Dub. Good game," Kevin replied, kissing her on the nose and patting her on the bum. Tory turned and sprinted upstairs to find a new activity for them. Kevin stood and walked slowly to the edge of the kitchen.

"Thanks for breakfast," Erin said, still chewing.

"You're welcome," Kevin replied, matter-of-factly. He sat down at the table and waited for her to finish. His face suddenly took on a heaviness, as if out of nowhere.

"Are you okay, honey?" Erin asked, looking concerned.

Kevin looked up at her slowly, then glanced away. "There's something I need to tell you." Kevin was about to speak when his attention turned to Tory, who ran into the room with her colouring books and crayons.

"You wanna colour, Daddy?" she asked, setting up a station at the table. "You can colour my zoo book." She added, trying to sweeten the deal.

"Maybe in a little while. Mommy and I need to talk about something first." Kevin replied. He suspected that they wouldn't get to colour together that day, but wasn't sure what else to say. He lowered his voice, turning to Erin, "Can we go upstairs?"

As Kevin closed the door of their bedroom, Erin felt a sinking feeling in her stomach. When things had started to improve between her and Kevin, she had pushed aside the fears and suspicions that she had harboured. Now they were all flooding back suddenly, as if she was awakening from a dream. As Kevin sat down beside her on the bed, she tried to swallow, but her throat was dry and her neck tight.

"First I have to tell you that, in the last little while, I've been so happy. Being with you feels like it used to. But before that . . . well you know that things weren't right. You felt it too. Neither of us was happy." Kevin paused and took two deep breaths, the second one accelerating. He felt panicked, unable to spit the words out. He closed his eyes tightly and pressed his hands into his thighs, rocking anxiously.

Erin's jaw tightened, sensing what was coming. She unclenched her teeth to prompt him reluctantly, "Just say it, Kevin." She stared at him intently, anticipating, already feeling hurt.

His face had already spoken the words that his mouth could not. He looked at Erin, pleading for forgiveness. "I never wanted to hurt you, Erin. I swear. I'd do anything to take it back, but I can't . . ."

"Who?" Erin interrupted, taking forced breaths, trying to hold herself together. Kevin looked at the floor, unable to respond. Erin shoved him hard on the shoulders with both hands, jolting him. "Who, Kevin?!" Her voice cracked, now consumed with fury, but still waiting for her answer.

"Just some girls on the road," Kevin responded quietly, like a child confessing. "But they didn't mean anything to me," Kevin added, thinking initially that it might be some consolation, realizing as the words came out that it would not.

"*Some* . . . girls on the road." Erin repeated. She was trembling, tears streaming down her cheeks. "*Some*?! You weren't sneaking cookies, Kevin, you were fucking other women!" Her voice rang off the walls, now elevated to screams of rage. Kevin flinched as she yelled.

He whispered back sheepishly, "Tory will hear you."

"Don't you shush me!" Erin snapped as she turned and walked to the door quickly. "Tory!" she called, as she hurried down the stairs. As she rounded the corner to the kitchen, she saw Tory standing in the middle of the room, trembling, struggling to breathe as she cried. Erin scooped her up and headed for the front door, with Kevin following.

"Erin, please." Kevin pleaded as he followed.

"Don't talk to me! I can't even look at you!" Erin barked as she pushed Tory's shoes onto her feet.

"Mommy, you're hurting me," Tory said, still crying.

"Erin, I'll do anything to fix this. Just . . . please stay." Kevin pleaded hopelessly as Erin grabbed Tory by the arm and pulled her out the door.

"Daddy?" Tory looked to Kevin, desperately confused.

"It'll be okay, sweetie. Just go with Mommy now. It'll be okay." Kevin attempted to reassure Tory and himself.

The tires squealed as the car pulled away. Kevin stood in the driveway alone, his hands cupped behind his neck, his forearms squeezing his head. He paced side to side helplessly, searching for hope, finding none. For the first time in his life, Kevin felt completely and utterly alone. He stumbled back into the house and dropped onto the couch, curling into a fetal position, rocking back and forth, his arms wrapped across his stomach. He was too overwhelmed, even to cry.

31

The house was silent. Several hours had passed. Kevin lay motionless on the couch, staring blankly at the wall. His eyes made their way around the perimeter of a frame, then settled on the image inside of it. The photo was a blow-up of his rookie hockey card. The eyes of the player were those of a warrior: aggressive, strong, and unafraid. His pads outlined a magnificent frame, one of power and prowess. Kevin exhaled from his nose sharply, the faintest sign of a laugh on his face. The image was in stark contrast to the way he saw himself now. He had cried for hours, shriveled up on the couch. He felt weak and exhausted, but above all, empty.

He was struck by the absurdity of the strength that he had always attempted to portray. It seemed illusory and superficial. What strength he had had over the years was intricately linked to a vulnerability that he had always fought. A vulnerability that he had always denied, always assumed that he would outgrow, until this moment. His true strength was drawn from those that loved him, those that had believed in him and supported him: his mother, Gord McCormack, Erin, and Tory. One had died, two had left, and he was too ashamed to tell his mother what had led him to this state.

Kevin's eyes explored the many photos around the room. Their faces told many stories. They painted a partial history, dictated primarily by hockey. As he looked, he remembered Cormie and the friendship that they had shared. He remembered the dreams that he and his little brother had shared, as his eyes scanned a childhood photo of them that Erin had only recently discovered and framed.

He saw the picture of Rick and himself after his first NHL goal, the puck mounted below, with Rick smiling like a proud father. Kevin noticed the rugged strength in Rick's face, even five years earlier. He wondered if Rick had come face to face with his own vulnerability. As he wondered, intuition answered his question. Rick had never hidden his priorities. He had never pretended that Kate and his girls were not the most important things in his life. He had never been affected by the teasing on the road about how much time he spent talking to them.

As Kevin looked at his wedding photo, he remembered seeing Gord and Lorna McCormack as he walked his new bride out of the church. Both were crying. Neither was trying not to. He had always seen in Cormie the qualities he wanted to see, ignoring the occasional signs of weakness or dependence that he saw. Now he was beginning to understand the foundation of those qualities. Cormie's strength and leadership in the game of hockey were *symptoms* of his true essence. Cormie knew that he needed Lorna. He knew that he needed people. He needed to love more than he needed to win. He needed.

Kevin sank back in the couch and reflected. For hours, he had been blinded by grief. Now he saw himself and his life with astonishing clarity. Hockey was just a game. But his family was his life. He had had more fun playing hockey in the last two games than he could ever remember. And why? His love for his wife had been rekindled. He had reconnected with his brother. He had salvaged his friendship with Rick. He had spent time with his dear friend, Gord McCormack, in the closing moments of his life. He had restructured his view of himself and the people around him. So hockey was fun again.

Now he sat alone, faced with the prospect of losing his wife and daughter. Now, as he scanned the multitude of hockey photos in his living room, they appeared empty. They seemed meaningless. He was faced with one simple and undeniable truth; playing hadn't allowed him to live. *Living* had allowed him to *play*.

But Kevin was afraid. He knew that it was possible that Erin might not come back. And now, more than ever, that idea terrified him. But he knew that she loved him. And he knew that she understood him better than anyone else in the world, especially now that Cormie was gone. If anyone could recognize that he was changing his ways for good, it would be Erin. But he knew that for now she had to be angry, that he would have to wait a while before any steps towards resolution would be taken. And what frightened him the most was the prospect of waiting alone.

Kevin was startled by the phone, not expecting Erin to call anytime soon, completely removed mentally from anyone else who might have called. He shifted painfully towards the table beside the couch to reach for the phone, not having moved for hours. "Hello?" he said quietly, hopeful that it might be her.

"Hey Kev, it's Rick."

Kevin sighed in disappointment, squinting from the throbbing of his head, "Hey. What's up?"

"I just wanted to let you know that Erin and Tory are here. I figured you'd be worried by now."

"Thanks, Olse. How's Erin?" Kevin asked, knowing that it probably wouldn't be good news.

"She was pretty upset, Kev. She was with Kate for quite a while, mostly crying. She's sleeping now."

"What about Tory?"

There was a pause on the line. "Well . . . she seemed pretty shaken up when they got here. Did she hear you guys fighting?" Rick asked, trying to make sense of it.

"Well . . . it wasn't much of a fight, but basically, yeah. How is she now?"

"Better, I think. She and Bethany are outside playing. She seems relatively content." Another long pause. "How are *you* holding up?"

"I've been better, but I think I'm starting to turn the corner. I knew it would be pretty rough, but I don't think you can ever really prepare yourself for something like this," Kevin said, resigned to his exhausted state.

"She's gonna need some time, Kev. Maybe a long time. But we'll take good care of her . . . and Tory."

"Thanks, Olse. That means a lot," Kevin replied, sounding a little relieved.

"You bet . . . You sure you're gonna be okay?" Rick asked, implying willingness to come over.

"Yeah. I'll let you know if I'm not," Kevin said, attempting to reassure his friend.

"Okay, Kev. Keep in touch. I'll do the same."

"Okay. Thanks for calling."

32

Two weeks later. The Olsen house.

Erin sat on the bathroom floor alone, sobbing. In her hand, she held a plastic stick with a pink handle. She glanced down again at the indicator window that revealed a blue line with unmistakable clarity. This was the second test that she had done. She was definitely pregnant.

Kate stood on the other side of the door, the lines on her forehead revealing her concern. "Erin? You okay, honey?"

Erin hurried to her feet, not realizing that Kate was home. "Sorry. I'll be out in a second."

"It's okay, honey. I just wanted to make sure you were okay." Kate continued, wanting to keep Erin talking until she was sure she was okay. "The girls are still at the park with Rick. I just came back to grab some juice boxes. You want to walk back over with me?" Kate asked hopefully, uncomfortable with the idea of leaving Erin alone for very long.

Erin opened the door and stood in the entrance. She was trying to speak but the words were trapped in her mouth. Instead, she held up the home pregnancy test for Kate to see, again starting to cry. Kate's head tilted slightly as she read Erin's face. She pulled Erin close to comfort her. As Erin cried, Kate rocked her gently from side to side, then held her by the shoulders and spoke. "Erin, listen. I know this is a difficult time, but don't miss the big picture. You've been blessed with another child. That's wonderful news, however things work out with Kevin. I won't let you turn this into bad news." Kate's voice was firm. She had listened to much of Erin's hurt and disappointment over the past two weeks and could no longer tolerate Erin's attempts to sustain them, especially not about this.

Erin took a deep breath and nodded. "You're right. I'm sorry, Kate." She realized after the fact that Kate had lost a baby, and would not be willing to see a pregnancy as anything but a gift. "Let me just wash my face and I'll come with you."

Kate nodded, her relief apparent in her eyes. "Good. I'll get the juice." As she walked to the fridge, Kate reflected on the two weeks that had passed. She had tried, gently at first, but more firmly of late, to help Erin to understand why Kevin might have made the decisions on the road that he had. She hadn't attempted to defend him, but wanted Erin to understand that it was something that could be put in the past if they were both committed to the future. Kate had been on the phone with Kevin periodically, and was proud of the patience and commitment that he had shown in giving Erin her space and not attempting to see her before she was ready.

Kate's own anger with Kevin had long since subsided. Now her frustration was with Erin who had fought hard to stay angry. Despite her attempts to be supportive, Kate had lost some respect for Erin, who continued to deflect Tory's inquiries about when she would see her daddy. Tory was still visibly confused and upset, missing him terribly. Kate had attempted to assure her that she would see him again soon, but Tory's trust in this reassurance was waning with each day that passed.

As the two women walked silently to the nearby playground, Kate reflected on events that marked the two years following her miscarriage. She recalled how weak and helpless she had felt, at the peak of her depression, as she tried to stay sympathetic to her friend. As Kate watched Erin and Tory play together in the park, Erin now looked especially small and fragile to her. It was a stark contrast from the courage that she had shown during her difficult pregnancy with Tory, even when her condition was considered to be potentially fatal. But then she fought because she had so much to live for. Now she had let go of that purpose, not because it was lost for good, but because the hurt prevented her from seeing it.

That evening, she was very quiet throughout dinner, contemplating what she finally decided she needed to tell Erin. Later, when the kids had been tucked in, she heard the guest room door close and headed down the hall. She knocked softly on the door. "Erin, can I come in?"

"Sure." Erin answered, curious about why she was there.

Kate walked in and sat on the edge of the bed. She paused, took a deep breath, and spoke, "Erin, I've tried to be a good friend and listen for the past several days without judging or pushing you to make a decision one way or the other. But I have some things that I feel I need to say, and I want you just to listen."

Erin leaned back against the headboard timidly, feeling like a little girl. "Okay."

"First of all, some guys don't deserve a second chance. They fool around until they get caught, then they do the song and dance to get their wives back, then go back to the same old behaviours. But I don't think that Kevin is one of those guys." Kate was relieved to see Erin's eyes come up, apparently listening openly to what she had to say. "Kevin told you what he had been doing. And I know it was terrible that he was cheating, but why do you think he came out and told you?" Erin shrugged.

Kate continued, "He obviously wasn't looking for a way out of the relationship. I've been on the phone with him every day, Erin, and he is crazy about you. He's willing to give you whatever you need to get through this. He hasn't even pushed the issue with Tory, and you know how he feels about her." Erin nodded, conceding the point.

"He understands how horrible this is for you, but he told you because he didn't want any more secrets. He felt guilty for accepting your love when you didn't have all the facts. He wanted to make things right. He's grown up a lot in the last little while, Erin. He's turning into the man that you were trying to save a month ago. And now it's killing me to see you willing to throw that away." Erin looked straight ahead, but the wells in her eyes told Kate that she was still listening.

"It's a shitty, shitty thing that he did, Erin. And it means that your marriage wasn't perfect, and neither is he, so you can let go of that idea because I could have told you that before any of this happened. But you know how great you two can be together. And you have a beautiful daughter together. And he's a wonderful, wonderful father. And now you're pregnant again. What are you losing by giving him another chance?"

The hurt came back over Erin's face as she reflected. "How can I ever forgive him for what he did, Kate? I know what we had was wonderful, but how do I know that he won't hurt me again if he's already shown that he can? How can I ever trust him again?"

Kate wiped a tear from her eye and sniffled as she listened. Then she looked Erin straight in the eyes and answered, "I don't know. Maybe you could ask Rick." Erin's eyes widened and she sat up straight, awaiting an explanation. Kate's tears began to flow, but she remained composed.

"After my miscarriage, I was depressed for months. Rick was devastated too, but he got through it by putting his energy into hockey, and reassuring himself and me that we'd get through it and there'd be other pregnancies. I didn't do as well. I pushed away and insisted on grieving for a long time, longer than he could understand. Eventually, he got frustrated and didn't try as hard to pull me out of it. I felt sorry for myself and got angry, isolating myself and, as a result, isolated him too." Erin listened intently, already in disbelief of what she was about to hear.

"I felt so alone that I was craving attention, craving any kind of closeness. Then one weekend when Meaghan was at her grandparent's and Rick was on the road, a guy that I knew from the gym asked me to go for a drink . . . so I went. After a few drinks, I started telling him my sob story and . . . we ended up in bed. Our bed. And I felt horrible. But the worse I felt, the more I craved some kind of comfort. And I didn't feel like I deserved Rick anymore, so I kept going back to this guy. Having him over to our house after Meaghan was asleep. Our house, Erin!"

Kate wiped her eyes and nose, trying to go on. "That's right. Rick had to somehow forgive me for sleeping with someone else . . . in *his* bed! With his daughter asleep down the hall. And I'm not sure how he did it. I'll never fully understand how or why he did it. But he did. And there isn't a day that goes by that I don't feel thankful for that second chance. Did I deserve it? I don't know, maybe not. But the one thing that I know for sure is that I would *never ever* do anything to hurt him again. And we've had the discussion enough times for me to tell you that he doesn't regret taking me back for a second. What we have now, it's wonderful, Erin. More wonderful than I ever believed possible. Is it perfect? No. But it never is. But we've got three little angels, and we have each other, . . . and we keep no secrets."

Kate stood up and walked to the door then turned to face Erin. "Goodnight, Erin." She closed the door behind her and walked to her bedroom. Rick was sitting in bed reading. He set down his book when she came in. He saw that she had been crying. "You told her about us?" Rick asked, fairly sure that he knew the answer.

Kate nodded and sniffled. Rick walked over and embraced her, holding her tight against his chest. He had long since forgiven her. Eight years had passed, but he wondered as he held her whether she would ever forgive herself.

33

In the back yard of the Wilkins' house, two men worked tirelessly in the sun, putting up a fence. Kevin and Brad Wilkins hadn't worked together on a project since their father had left, ten years earlier. It had been the closest link that they had to their father, a carpenter, other than his excitement about their hockey exploits.

The radio played on a portable stereo, and Brad wondered if Kevin was listening to the words of the Hootie & the Blowfish song, which might be striking a chord, under the circumstances:

> *Let her cry, let the tears fall down like rain,*
> *Let her sing, if it eases all her pain,*
> *Let her go, let her walk right out on me,*
> *And if the sun comes up tomorrow, let her in.*

Kevin stopped working for a moment and looked around on the grass. "Uh oh, where'd he go? Is he over there with you, Brad?"

At the other corner of the yard, Brad replied, smiling, "Yep. He's crashed against the tree here. Totally passed out." Kevin walked over to see. A tiny Labrador Retriever puppy lay with his face pressed against the base of a tree, eyes closed, with his little round belly rising gently with each breath. With time on his own, Kevin had given in to a whim while wandering through a pet store in the mall. In retrospect, it seemed like a pretty constructive solution, considering the difficulty he had in being alone. He named the puppy 'Gordie'.

Since then, he'd had more company. Brad had offered to come and spend a few weeks with him. He attempted to disguise it as an off-season training trip, but the training wasn't to start until the next week, so Kevin had no illusions about Brad's intentions. And he greatly appreciated them.

They had spent the week building the fence in the day, chatting and playing with the puppy at night. Brad was amazed at how open and reflective Kevin was about his life, especially with respect to his marriage, his mistakes, and the shift in perspective that he'd been having of late. They had never truly 'talked' as kids, but the three-year age difference seemed negligible now.

Brad seemed apologetic when he talked about Carla and how excited he was about their relationship. But Kevin continued to ask questions, and smiled thoughtfully as he listened to each little anecdote. It felt good to be around someone who was so happy.

Kevin and Brad stood back to inspect their work, content that the job had been done well. "Not bad, little brother," Kevin proclaimed.

"Not bad at all," Brad responded. "Just have to do the gate and paint 'er up."

"Lunch?" Kevin prompted.

"Yeah, what do you feel like?" Brad asked.

"Well, we could finish off that pasta from last night, but there's not that much of it." Kevin suggested, hoping for a better idea.

"Why don't I zip over to Quiznos? You can stay here with Gordie."

"Sure, if you don't mind going. I'll get some money," Kevin insisted, as he headed inside.

"No, let me get this, Kev. You've paid for my whole trip."

Kevin grabbed Brad's hand and placed a twenty in his palm, then looked him in the eyes appreciatively, "I don't think I could ever repay what you've given me this week, Brad."

Brad shrugged modestly, "I just came and hung out, did a little work on a fence."

"Right." Kevin smiled.

Brad paused, then sighed, realizing that nothing more needed to be said. "What kind of sub do you want?"

"Um . . . they usually have a special goin'. Surprise me."

"Gotcha. Back in a bit." Brad grabbed the keys to the jeep and headed for the door. Kevin walked out the back to go get Gordie and bring him in. He paused for one last look at the little guy, before scooping him up. As he started to bend down, he heard a voice behind him. He froze for a second, trying to determine whether he'd just imagined it.

"Daddy!!" Tory's voice filled the yard, as she came running toward Kevin. Gordie came to with a start, and looked around in a panic for an escape route as the little girl sprinted towards him. Kevin dropped to his knees in time for Tory to throw herself at him. They embraced for several seconds. Kevin felt a sensation of wholeness as Tory's tiny arms squeezed him around his neck. Almost whole. Kevin opened his eyes to see Erin standing timidly in the opening of the sliding door. She choked back her tears as she saw her daughter and husband together again, swimming in a mix of guilt, relief, joy, and residual anger.

Gordie inched his way back towards Kevin from the corner of the yard, sensing that he might not be in any immediate peril. Tory let herself down from Kevin and looked over at Gordie, her eyes drawing wide as she focused in on the tiny lab. Her voice failed her as she tried to verbalize the discovery. "A puppy."

"Yeah sweetie, that's our new puppy. His name's Gordie."

Tory squatted down slowly, instinctively trying to comfort the startled pup. Gordie walked cautiously towards her, sniffed her hand, then nuzzled under her arm, now seeking comfort from the person that had startled him. Both Kevin and Erin were transfixed on the two of them together. Tory massaged his floppy ears, while Gordie walked up the front of her, trying to lick her face.

Kevin stood up, looking at Erin. She looked back at him, fighting tears, then glanced at the puppy, as if to inquire about it. Kevin shrugged, looking embarrassed. "Impulse buy." Erin smiled widely, almost laughing, and tilted her head slightly, almost in pity, wondering what other surprises had come out of her absence.

Kevin sat down on the patio bench, unsure if he could come any closer. "Brad's here," he said, trying to break the awkward silence.

"I know. I saw him on the way in." Her face grew serious. "I'm still feeling really hurt, Kev. I mean . . . I'm still mad at you."

"I'm still mad at me too," Kevin assured her.

"And you're going to have to be patient with me, so I can get over this . . ."

"I will, Erin. Whatever it takes."

"Okay . . ." Erin nodded, trying to coax herself along, "I'd like to try again."

As she saw a tear make its way down Kevin's cheek, Erin felt a wave of emotion come over her and stepped out onto the patio, towards Kevin. She stopped herself, and looked longingly up at him. He was frozen, not knowing what to do. Finally, Erin's face took on an expression of complete resignation and she stumbled into Kevin's arms. They both cried and held each other tightly.

Erin's anger was drowned out by relief, feeling like the one person who could comfort her was the person who had hurt her in the first place. She had abandoned her game plan of not touching him. Her need to be held by him became overwhelming. She was angry and hurt, and relieved, and accepted . . . and loved. For no objective reason, she felt in her heart a confidence that they would get through this challenge. She didn't scrutinize it, just gave in to it.

Each of them felt a tiny arm wrap around their leg. Tory had joined in the hug. It had been a long two weeks for her. Gordie got up on his hind legs, leaning a front paw on Kevin's leg, attempting to see what all the fuss was about.

There was work to be done to restore trust, to repair hurt feelings. But this moment restored their hope. Together, the three of them felt whole. They felt complete. They would need this feeling if they were ever to heal completely.

34

The weeks that followed were tiring for both Kevin and Erin. Together they recounted the previous couple of years, trying to assess how the damage had occurred for both of them. Kevin shared with her the insights that Cormie had provided. Erin was relieved by the amount of responsibility that Kevin took for losing his way. Erin gradually assembled in her head what details she felt she needed to hear about Kevin's infidelity, in order to put it to rest. Eventually they formed intentions about how they would provide each other with what they needed, and what they wanted.

Brad offered to leave, but Erin insisted that he stay. Kevin had left that decision up to her, insisting that she have whatever conditions made her most comfortable. Having Brad there provided a reprieve from the heaviness of their private discussions. He was also happy to spend time with Tory, to spell them off periodically.

And so it went, for a couple of weeks. Kevin and Brad would train together in the mornings. Erin took on painting the new fence as a project to busy herself, while Tory took care of Gordie. In the afternoons, the four of them would usually find a park to go to or take the boat out around the nearby islands with a picnic lunch, with Tory clutching Gordie tightly to keep him from wandering overboard.

Despite the strides that she and Kevin had made in rebuilding their relationship and an open line of communication, Erin was relieved when Carla came for Brad's last week with them. She was happy to have a girlfriend to chat with while the boys were being boys, or talking hockey. She also wanted to give Kate some time away from her, deciding in retrospect that she must have been a lot to take in those couple of weeks.

One morning, while the boys were training, Carla drew a link that Erin hadn't considered. They'd had enough open discussions for her to bring it up. "You know how you described the way you and Kev became very distant from each other?" Erin nodded. "Well, I wonder if that's how it happened for Susan and their dad. I mean . . . I'm not saying it was bound to happen, but maybe that's where Kevin saw it first."

Erin sat silently, trying to replay Kevin's descriptions of how his parents had split up. "He never really talked about the time leading up to it. But maybe you're right."

Carla continued her train of thought. "Well, Brad said he had to get used to how 'huggy' I was, because his folks were never like that. I just wonder if they stopped being that way at some point. Maybe that's when their dad started to see that other woman."

Erin stared off in the distance thoughtfully. "You know, it's funny. I knew that he left with another woman, but I'd never really thought about how it might have come about . . . hm."

"Well, Kevin sure seems determined to set his own course now," Carla stated surely. Erin looked at her, nodding slightly, but hoping for some elaboration. "Brad said his old coach gave him a pretty good shake. He turned himself around, but needed to clear the slate, give you the choice of forgiving him or not."

Erin smiled faintly, then squinted, giving in to another thought, "But sometimes I just can't shake the image of him with another woman. I just . . . that's really hard." She exhaled heavily, looking to Carla for some validation.

Carla nodded knowingly. "My mom caught my dad in bed with my dance instructor in Hungary." Erin's eyes widened in disbelief. Carla continued, "I know. I can't imagine. She didn't tell me until a few years ago. I remember being so mad when she made me switch academies. Anyway, somehow she got past it." A smile came over her face. "They're so cute together now. So passionate."

Erin sat quietly, a little deflated at the implication that women were expected to forgive such transgressions. Then Carla offered her some relief. "I would have left." Both women laughed.

Then Erin probed Carla for some deeper consideration. "Do you ever worry that it might happen with Brad?"

Carla nodded. "Mm hm, sometimes." She looked far away for a moment. "Brad was shocked when Kevin called and told him what he had done. He was always telling me how you guys were this perfect couple . . . just totally meant to be. He said that when we got together, he was no longer envious of Kevin, because he finally had that too. But I'm not so naïve as to believe that the same thing couldn't happen to us. I just take it as a reminder that you never get complacent, you never stop working at it."

"So how do you do that?" Erin asked, seeking insight.

"Well, when I got engaged, my mother said, 'Csinibaba', that's what she calls me. It means 'pretty baby', 'Csinibaba' she said, 'pay attention to what you need to feel complete, to feel like a woman. And ask him what he needs often enough that if it changes, you can change what you give. You can either give each other the freedom of happiness or the trappings of sadness. The first one can happen if you do the work. The second . . . well, it can happen all by itself.' That's the loose translation, anyway. It seemed a little heavy as a response to my good news, but it certainly stuck with me."

Erin nodded, impressed by the wisdom of Carla's mother. She sat back and sipped her lemonade, quietly accepting that the work that she and Kevin were doing now would have to be a work in progress. She snapped out of her trance, and smiled warmly at Carla. "Thanks for coming. It's really nice having you here."

Carla smiled back, then returned the sentiment the best way she knew how. She hopped out of her chair and pulled Erin out of hers to give her a proper hug, spilling a little of her lemonade. "Well, we're sisters now. We're going to be seeing lots of each other."

Tory came running out onto the patio, Gordie close behind her. "Mommy, Carla, I have to show you my dance." Both women sat back down, directing their full attention to Tory on the lawn/dance floor. She plugged in her tiny stereo and began leaping around the lawn to the sounds of her Pocahontas tape, with Gordie nipping at her heals playfully. "Gordie, no!" She exclaimed as she approached the finale, "Gordie, not now!" Erin and Carla pressed their lips together, trying not to giggle.

At the conclusion, Tory curtsied, as she'd been taught, and Carla exclaimed, "That was beautiful, Csinibaba." Tory looked up at her blankly. "That's your new nickname, Tory. That's what my mommy calls me."

Tory smiled, but her nose scrunched up at the sound of it. Then Tory gathered herself, trying to be polite, "Oh . . . okay."

35

Broadcast booth. GM Place. Eight months later.

"After two periods of play, the Canucks lead the Bluejackets of Columbus 3-1. The story of this game, as has been the case all season, would have to be the dominant play of Kevin Wilkins. With assists on all three Vancouver goals, he moves ahead of Philadelphia's Cosic in the points race with 59, putting him five points back of the leader, Sporkowsky of Detroit."

"Well, Canucks' assistant Jamie Harris was talking before the game about the patience and creativity that Wilkins seems to have with the puck this year. He had a lot of success in the past with a straight power, speed, crash and bang style, but this new element in his game has really taken him to another level. Despite a concussion scare in the preseason, Wilkins has been unstoppable. He's on pace for about forty goals again, but his assists have almost doubled from this time last year."

"And Chris, if you're Vlad Koshenko, you couldn't be happier about that. He leads all scorers with thirty-one goals, and we're just past the half way point of the season. Here you can see that patience that Wilkins has with the puck on the two-on-one. He waits, and he waits, then flips it over the D-man's stick to Koshenko for an easy tap-in on the Canucks' third goal, Koshenko's second of the game."

"The sub-plot that we featured in the pre-game show has also been fun to watch. Kevin Wilkins' younger brother, Brad, or 'Little Wilk' as he's been re-nicknamed from his junior days, continues to impress for the Bluejackets, scoring their only goal on the powerplay, to pull them back within two."

"Well, head coach Marty Schick told me in the off-season that he had the best-kept scouting secret he'd ever had coming to camp. He said that not only does this kid have the potential to be a stand-out in this league, but he could step in and play right away."

"And that he has, Curt, scoring his twelfth tonight, with seven of those coming on the power play. But I'm impressed with his toughness. He had that skirmish with Soles, late in the period, and showed no interest in backing down. He doesn't have the stature of his older brother, but he appears to be every bit the warrior."

In the Canucks' locker room, the players joked. "Hey Wilk, tell your little brother to quit pickin' on Solesy." Billy said mockingly.

Soles barked a reply to try to save face. "He's a tough little guy, Wilk, . . . what happened to you?" The other players oooed at the cut.

"Well, I used to be that tough, Solesy, but . . . ever since I started dating your mom, I just don't have the heart anymore." The room erupted, despite the generic form of the comeback. Sometimes timing is everything.

Jamie Harris walked quickly into the locker room and straight to Kevin. "Um, Wilk, . . . I'm not even sure I should be telling you this right now, but . . . Erin just went into labour." Kevin looked up at Harris, his eyes wide. Harris knew his fears were about to be confirmed.

Moments later, the coaches sat in Marcel Boucher's office, discussing adjustments on the penalty kill. Boucher caught a glimpse of Kevin running past the open door in his street clothes. "Was that Wilk?" Boucher asked in disbelief. He jumped out of his seat and ran out of the office in pursuit. "Wilk!" Boucher got to main door of the team rooms in time to watch Kevin disappear around the corner in the rounded corridor. "Wilk! Wilk!!" Boucher turned to the other coaches who had come out of the office to see what was going on. "God Damn it! . . . Where's he goin'?"

In a delivery room, Erin was breathing through her contractions, squeezing Kate's hand tightly. "You're doing great, Erin. Just keep breathing."

"Is . . . Kev . . . coming?" Erin asked rhythmically with her breaths.

"He'll be here as soon as he can, honey. Just focus on your breathing." As she spoke, Kevin ran into the room.

"Woah, woah, woah!" the nurse barked at him like a protective terrier.

Kevin held up his hand, "I'm the father. I'm the father," he explained, struggling to catch his breath. "Hey Erin. . . . How's it going? What'd I miss?" He grabbed her hand, and Erin looked up at him in relief, now between contractions.

"Lots of time yet, Kev. Better take your jacket off and get comfortable." Kate suggested.

"I'm okay like this, Kate. . . . Thanks." Kevin replied, not wanting to let go of Erin's hand. "I ran into the wrong room back there," Kevin said, pointing over his shoulder. "A little more than I wanted to see," he added, laughing nervously.

"Oh, don't make me laugh," Erin insisted.

"Oh, okay, sorry. How is everything? The baby's okay? Everything looks okay?" Kevin asked, all in one breath.

Erin nodded, "The doctor said everything looks great. Oh . . . uhoh." Erin started another contraction.

Kevin's eyes widened in panic, raising his hand above his head, as if reaching for the right response, "Oh, um, ah, ah, breathe! Breathe, Erin. Like we did in class!" Erin was already ahead of him. Kate giggled quietly to herself at the sight of a professional athlete overwhelmed with anxiety.

As the labour wore on, Kevin settled in, eventually taking off his jacket. He coached and encouraged, holding Erin's hand the whole time. Fear and anxiety gave way to pure excitement and joy, inspired by Erin's strength. He cried throughout, but made no attempts not to. It all happened very quickly, within an hour and a half of Kevin's arrival. As the baby's tiny hips slid out, the mystery was unveiled. "A boy, Erin. It's a boy! It's a boy!" Kevin exclaimed excitedly.

When the doctor handed the baby to his father, Kevin was trembling, trying to focus through the tears at the little person in his hands. "He's beautiful, Erin. He's got your little nose."

"Can I see him, Kev?" Erin squeaked. "Come down here, we'll hold him together."

Kate stood back, also in tears, suddenly flashing back to the events in the spring, when Erin and Kevin's future hung in the balance. Her arms were wrapped around her body, hugging herself, overjoyed by the miracle that she had again witnessed, warmed by the confidence that life has a funny way of working out.

A little while later, Erin and baby were wheeled out of the delivery room and down the hall. Tory stood in the hall on her tiptoes, trying to get a good look at her new sibling. Minutes later, the whole family sat huddled together in a room. The baby squawked quietly, adjusting to the outside world.

Tory sat, transfixed on her little brother. "What's his name, Mommy?" Erin looked up at Kevin seeking confirmation that they would go with the name that they'd agreed upon. Kevin nodded, smiling widely.

"His name is Connor. Connor Gordon Wilkins," Erin stated proudly.

"That's a good name," Tory said approvingly, never taking here eyes off of him. "Hi Connor. Welcome to Vancouver," Tory said, grandly, as if he'd just gotten off a plane.

A couple more minutes passed, and there was a knock at the door. "Heard you guys were expanding your roster," Brad said as he poked his head in.

"Brad!" Kevin said in surprise. "I thought you'd be on a plane."

"I was able to get a flight out first thing tomorrow. It's only an hour to Calgary," he explained as he bent over to kiss Erin on the cheek.

"Who won, anyway?" Kevin asked, barely interested.

"Um, you guys, 3-2," Brad replied, having to think about it. "So what's his name?" Brad continued.

"Connor Gordon Wilkins," Tory announced.

"Gordon," Brad said, looking at Kevin knowingly. A smirk came over his face, "After the dog?"

36

Three weeks later. Pengrowth Saddledome, Calgary.

Kevin showered quickly after the morning skate in Calgary. The other players were chatting and joking in the dressing room, but Kevin was conspicuously uninvolved in the chatter. He dressed without a word and headed for the door. He stopped in the corridor to talk to Jamie Harris. "Bones, I won't be on the bus. I've got to do something right near the Dome here. I'll catch a cab to the hotel."

"Sure, Wilk. Will you be back for the pre-game meal?" Harris asked, hoping to preserve Kevin's game day routine.

"I'll try," Kevin responded, patting Harris on the shoulder and heading down the hall.

In the locker room, Billy came out of the shower, scanning the room. "Wilk gone already?" he asked curiously to whomever was listening.

"Yeah, he just left," Rick replied.

"Where'd he go?" Billy inquired.

"Um . . . I'm not sure," Rick answered hesitantly, thinking he knew, but choosing to keep it to himself.

Just a few blocks south of the Saddledome, Kevin found the cemetery that Lorna had directed him to. He studied the hand-drawn map that he had sketched over the phone and made his way to the back of the grounds. As he walked, he wondered if the proximity of the cemetery to the last place Cormie ever coached was coincidental, doubting that it was.

He slowed down as he neared the 'x' on his map, then scanned the ground, spotting a small stone bearing Cormie's name. It was not fancy or extravagant. Simple but pleasant looking. *Very Cormie*, Kevin thought. The snow had been cleared off of it, without the snow around it being disturbed . . . very Lorna. His heart skipped as he read the full inscription:

Gordon Ellis McCormack
"Cormie"
December 2ⁿᵈ, 1943-April 6ᵗʰ, 2001
"From all those whose lives you touched:
You'll be in our hearts forever."

Kevin squatted down in front of it and began to speak. "This is the second time I have to do all the talking," Kevin said with a half laugh, sobered by the lonely silence that was Cormie's reply.

"Things are going great, Cormie. I took all your advice. I made things right with Erin. It was tough, but we got through it. Tory's four now. She's already reading. Some days I think she's already smarter than me. Got that from Erin, I guess. We've got a new little guy, Connor Gordon, . . . after you." Kevin's voice broke.

He sniffled, wiped his eyes, took a deep breath, and continued. "He doesn't do much yet, but he's awesome. Erin wrote a children's book about nutrition. It's called *Keeps Me Growin', Keeps Me Goin'*. It's pretty cool. She's already sold a bunch of them to the schools. I patched things up with Brad. We're like best friends now. He's married now. You'd love his wife. She's a lot like you in some ways. Every day is a celebration of life for her. I think she's rubbing off on Erin and me. Brad's in Columbus, doing awesome. Hockey's going great for me right now too . . . maybe because it's a *game* again, like you said. I've only talked to Lorna a couple of times since . . . we last talked. Sorry about that. I'll be better about keeping in touch from now on."

Kevin set a tiny frame in front of the stone. Inside was a picture of Connor, tiny and pink, that was taken at the hospital. "Anyway, here's a picture of the little guy. I figured you'd want a copy." Kevin took a couple of deep breaths, trying to collect himself, then spoke his final thoughts. "I miss you, Cormie. . . . I'll talk to you later."

He pushed on his knees, standing up slowly. As he turned, he was startled by the presence of someone standing behind him. "Lorna. Geez, you scared me."

"Sorry, Kevin. I didn't want to interrupt," Lorna responded, trying to explain her silence.

Kevin shook his head, "Don't be sorry." He gave her a hug and a kiss on the cheek. "It's good to see you."

"You too, Kevin. I keep hearing about how well you're doing," she said proudly.

"Oh . . . who were you talking to?" Kevin looked surprised. "Oh, you mean with hockey." Lorna nodded, surprised that there would be any uncertainty. "Yeah, things are pretty good. Could move into a fifth place tie in the conference with a win tonight." Lorna smiled, still delighting in his excitement about the game. "How are you doing, Lornie?" Kevin couldn't hide the pity in his voice.

"Good days and bad. Christmas was a pretty emotional time. But I'm surviving." She nodded as she spoke, trying to reassure him.

"You come here very often?" Kevin asked, not sure why.

"Some weeks more than others. They tell me the first year is the toughest. I hope it's true," Lorna said, wanting to share with him a hint of what she'd been through.

"I'm sure it is," Kevin paused uncomfortably. "Oh, I left a picture of Connor there," he said, pointing. "Did you get yours?"

"Yes, it came just yesterday. He's going to be handsome like his father," Lorna said warmly. Kevin smiled shyly, a little embarrassed by the compliment.

"Well, I should actually get back to the hotel for the pre-game meal," Kevin said apologetically.

"Of course, dear. I'm going to stay for a while."

"It was nice to see you, Lornie. I'll call you again soon . . . I promise," Kevin said, looking her right in the eyes.

"That would be lovely, Kevin. Say hi to Erin and Tory for me." Kevin nodded and turned, walking back down the path and off the grounds.

37

Three months later.

"We're here at Joe Louis Arena in Detroit in what is shaping up to be a preview of the first round play-off match-up between these two teams. It appears unlikely that either team will catch the 3rd place Stars in the standings, or be caught by the 6th place Oilers making a first round meeting probable. The fans seem to sense the importance of this game, as home ice advantage is on the line."

"And if that's not exciting enough, Paul, the top three point-getters in the league are all here tonight: Dale Sporkowsky of the Red Wings continues to dazzle as the runaway leader of the scoring race. But the Canucks will look to their stars, Kevin Wilkins and Vladimir Koshenko, to do their damage in the offensive zone."

In the locker room, the Canuck players were quieter and more focused than was typical of most regular season games. Kevin sat quietly, absorbing the energy of the players around him. As game time drew closer, the chatter began.

"Be tough in the D-zone fellas. Don't give them anything for free. Let's suffocate them, frustrate them," Rick started.

"Let's put Sporkowsky on his ass too, boys. He can't try any of his fancy shit from his back. Hey, Kopper?!" Billy added. Kyle Kopp nodded emphatically, still looking straight ahead.

Harris poked his head in the room. "Two minutes, boys. Two minutes to show-time."

The players made their way to the corridor. Kevin shrugged off a little nervous tension, bouncing slightly on the spot. Vlad walked over and stood beside him, glancing up at him and nodding, as if to suggest that this was their show, their game to make or break. Kevin winked at him and smiled, then smacked Billy on the shin pads with his stick. "Let's set the tone out there. Big first shift." Both linemates nodded in agreement.

The first five minutes was all Vancouver, with the Detroit players scrambling to match the torrid pace that had been set. The first line seemed able to penetrate the Detroit zone at will, challenging Rubik, the Detroit goalie early. But the game remained scoreless.

Corey Lynch brought the Canuck bench to its feet with a punishing open ice hit on the usually-evasive Dale Sporkowsky. A scrum ensued, with the Detroit players sending the message that their star was not fair game for heavy hits. But the second line players kept their cool enough to earn the man-advantage.

The first line took the ice for the power play. Koshenko won the face-off back to Kopp who gained the center line and slapped the puck into the Detroit zone. Billy raced at the Detroit defender forcing him to try to clear the puck out quickly. It was knocked down by Kopp at the line and the Canucks began working the puck around for an open shot. Kevin battled in front of the net, resisting the cross-checks of the Detroit player trying to move him. Kyle Kopp waited for an open lane and one-timed a shot towards the net. Kevin got a piece of the shot with his stick, sending it over Rubik's shoulder for the first goal.

Detroit coach, Owen Massey, called from the bench. "Come on, we've got to move him! He's not *that* strong! Baker, if you can't handle him, tell me! I'll get someone out there who can!"

Detroit slowly began to match the intensity of Vancouver, but continued to struggle in containing the high-powered first line. Billy and Kevin were relentless, battering the Detroit defense at every opportunity. Koshenko moved the puck around the Detroit defensemen like they were pylons, but Lukas Rubik kept his team in the game with save after save.

Coach Massey grew increasingly exasperated, "Get a body on those guys! They're killin' us! They're killin' us, men!" The Detroit bench was visibly rattled by the onslaught of the Vancouver first-liners.

Kevin fished the puck out of the corner and whistled a pass in front of the net that was tapped just wide by Billy. Billy hustled behind the net, knocking the Detroit defender off the puck, tipping it around the boards to Kevin. Kevin ducked out of the way of a check, spinning out of the corner again. But as he turned, Detroit defenseman, Sheldon Baker threw a check at him, with elbows raised as he exploded into him. Kevin's head snapped back, taking the full brunt of an elbow. His body went limp as he fell back onto the ice.

Billy rushed at Baker, dropping his gloves and stick and pouncing on top of him throwing punches furiously. A pile formed over Baker and Morrison, as tempers flared on both sides. Meanwhile, Kevin lay motionless, a few feet away.

While the linesmen struggled to separate the two sides, Detroit goaltender Lukas Rubik glided around the pile to get a better look at Kevin's status. He quickly raised his stick, waving at the Vancouver bench for medical attention. Trainer, Tony Paxton, was already on the ice, hustling over to Kevin.

From the bench, Rick watched nervously, waiting for Kevin to show some signs of consciousness, unable to go look because of the brawl that was still in progress. One linesman eventually wrestled Billy off of Baker, but Billy continued trying to get at him, still in a fit of rage. "You're mine, Baker! I'm gonna rip your fuckin' head off!"

Paxton was now kneeling over Kevin, speaking into both ears, trying to get some response. Nothing. He took off Kevin's glove, pinching his fingers. Still nothing. He took out Kevin's mouth guard, careful not to move his head, then cleared his airway with his fingers. "Okay, looks like he's breathing." He checked the pulse in his neck. "And we've got a pulse," Paxton coached himself along.

Kevin's eyes opened and he began to cough, spitting up a little. Paxton's eyes widened, startled but relieved, then wiped the small amount of vomit from Kevin's mouth. The Detroit medical staff were now on the ice with them, ready to assist.

"Okay, Kevin, can you hear me?" Paxton continued.

"Yeah." Kevin replied with a half cough, as he started to lift his head.

"Woah, woah, Wilk, put your head down, okay. I want you to stay as still as you can. Do you have any pain in your neck?" Paxton asked, carrying on automatically.

"No, it's fine," Kevin replied.

"Okay, great. Can you tell me my name?" Paxton continued.

Kevin's eyes strained to make out the blurred figure above him, struggling to make out the face to match the voice that he knew well. "I know it's you, Pax."

"Okay, great, Kev. Do you know where we are?"

Kevin again strained to see, unable to make out the details of the building above him, searching his memory in vain. "No . . . St. Louis?"

"No Wilk, we're in Detroit," Paxton corrected, digesting the seriousness of the concussion.

The Detroit physician leaned over, "Can I check his neck?" Paxton nodded, relieved to have the help. "Kevin, tell me if you have any pain as I do this." He pressed each vertebrae in Kevin's neck.

"No, it's fine." Kevin said, still groggy.

"And nothing in your back?"

"No."

The doctor went through a series of quick tests to confirm that there was no damage to the spine. "Okay, let's get a soft collar on him, then we'll turn him, in case he throws up again." he continued. At the mention of throwing up, Kevin tasted the noxious film on his teeth, and felt his stomach turn. His body contracted as he threw up again, just seconds after he'd been turned on his side. His eyes watered and his breathing accelerated, starting to feel panicked by his condition. "Everything's blurry, Pax. Everything's . . . blurry." Kevin blinked hard, trying to orient himself, then put his head back down.

"Listen, Wilk. We're gonna get you on the stretcher and get you to the hospital. Okay? Just relax and don't try to move."

Kevin nodded slightly, wishing that he hadn't.

"Keep your head still though, Wilk," Paxton insisted.

By now, the paramedics were on the scene, cautiously sliding Kevin onto the stretcher and raising it to its wheels. Kevin looked up, able to make out Rick's face above him. "Hey, Kev. I'll come see you right after the game. Okay, buddy? You just try to stay relaxed, they'll take good care of you."

As they lifted Kevin's stretcher from the ice, Rick had a sudden image of Erin watching at home flash through his head. He hurried down the corridor to the locker room, fishing in his jacket for his cell phone. He dialed quickly, then waited nervously for an answer.

"Hello?"

Rick paused, trying to remember what number he had dialed. "Kate? I was trying to call Erin."

"She's here. We're having kind of a girls' night, just hanging out with the baby. Aren't you supposed to be playing right now?" Kate asked, a little confused. "It's Rick," she whispered to Erin.

"You guys don't have the game on?" Rick asked trying to assess their knowledge of what had happened.

"No, the girls are watching a movie. Why? What's happened?" Kate's face grew worried.

"Kevin got hit hard. He was unconscious for a couple of minutes."

"Oh my God," Kate reacted.

Erin looked up from Connor with concern. "What? Is it Kev?"

Rick tried to reassure, hearing Erin in the background. "He's conscious now. It looks like he's gonna be fine. But they're taking him to the hospital."

Erin held out her hand for the phone. "Can I talk to him?" Kate held out the phone nervously.

"Rick? What's going on?" Erin asked, in a shaky voice.

"Erin. Listen. Kev's gonna be okay, but he's had another concussion. This one's worse than the others, but he's conscious now and they're taking him to the hospital to make sure he gets the attention he needs." Erin covered her mouth, fighting to maintain her composure. "Erin, I'll call you again as soon as I know more. . . . Can I talk to Kate again, real quick?"

Erin passed the phone back, starting to shake, rocking Connor nervously side to side.

"Kate, stay there with her, okay? I'll call back when I get to the hospital. It won't be for a while. We're still in the first."

"Okay, I'll stay here," Kate agreed.

"It was scary, Kate. I just . . . I'm just glad you guys didn't have the game on."

Kate took a deep breath, trying not to respond out loud to what Rick had just said. "Okay, I'll talk to you later then," she said as a cover. She turned off the phone and moved onto the couch with Erin, putting her arm around her to console her. "He'll be okay, Erin. He'll be okay."

38

Kevin was sitting up in his hospital bed listening to Rick's account of what had happened. His last memories were from the game in St. Louis, two nights before. His face was expressionless as he listened. Rick stopped and looked into Kevin's glassy eyes. "How are you feeling now, Kev?"

Kevin's eyes were stuck in a trance, as he answered slowly. "Pretty . . . pretty out of it. My head's really achy, so I'm just trying to stay as still as possible."

Rick looked worried as he listened, probing for some encouraging signs, "Still nauseous?"

"No. So that's good at least," Kevin said with a sigh, still staring straight ahead.

Rick wondered what the implications of this concussion would be on Kevin's ability to play again, then chastised himself mentally for looking too far ahead. Jamie Harris sat in the corner quietly, spooked by Kevin's distant state. Rick and Jamie looked at each other, each knowing what the other was thinking. This was Kevin's fifth concussion in two seasons, and this one felt different. They both had a bad feeling.

Billy walked into the room excitedly. "Hey, there he is. How you feeling, buddy?"

Kevin's head turned slowly to see him. He looked over blankly and spoke, "Not great." Billy looked at Rick and Jamie, his face registering more worry than Rick thought he was capable of. The 'Wilk' that they knew was not in that room. The man that they were with was vacant and fragile. His blank expression was telling clinically, but these three men that were there to see him saw more in his eyes: distance, pain, fear, resignation.

The on-call doctor came in with Tony Paxton along side of him. "Kevin?" he prompted, knowing that he might have to say it more than once to get his attention.

"Mm hm," Kevin replied quietly.

"We're going to keep you overnight for observation. Tony here said he'll arrange for you to see your team doctors when you get home. This was not your standard 'bell-ringing'. You're going to have to be very careful with this one. Probably will have to make some tough decisions in the next little while." Kevin nodded, although what the doctor was hinting at was not really registering. "You definitely won't want to do much of anything until you're symptom-free . . . and that may be a while."

Harris stood up and walked to the side of Kevin's bed. "Just take good care of yourself, okay Kevin. We'll talk when you get home. We've got to catch the plane."

Rick put his hand on Kevin's shoulder. "I'll call Erin and explain everything when I get outside . . . I can't use my phone in here."

Kevin nodded slowly. "Thanks, Olse."

Billy's turn. He was clearly rattled, searching for something to say. "See ya at home, buddy. You'll be back for play-offs. Don't worry."

Kevin wasn't worried about the play-offs. He was worried about the pounding in his head, wondering if it would ever subside. He was worried about his vision, which was still blurry and very light-sensitive. He was tired, and frustrated that the nurses would not let him go to sleep.

Outside the hospital, Rick dialed Erin's number again. She answered immediately. "Hello?"

"Hi, Erin. Me again. I just saw him. He was sitting up and talking. Still pretty groggy though." Rick explained.

"Is he gonna be okay?" Erin asked impatiently.

"They're going to keep him here overnight for observation. They'll know more tomorrow, they said. Try to get some rest, Erin. He'll probably be back tomorrow, but if he is, they'll want you to watch him pretty closely."

"Thanks, Rick." Erin responded softly, almost in a whisper.

"Okay, talk to you soon." Rick said, closing the call.

Erin hung up and looked over at Kate, trying to hold herself together. Kate saw the desperation in her eyes, unable to do anything from so far away.

"You want us to stay, Erin?" Kate offered.

Erin shook her head, "No. The kids have school tomorrow. You'd better go."

Kate woke Bethany and Kayla, who were already asleep in the guest room. Erin saw them to the door, for a round of hugs. Kate whispered as she hugged, "I'll talk to you tomorrow." Erin nodded and gave her an extra squeeze of thanks.

She waved as they pulled away, then stood at the door, suddenly feeling very alone. In the past year, she and Kevin had rebuilt the foundation that they had once had. They had rebuilt their love for each other and the meaning that they found in being together, and needing each other. They were integrally linked to each other's purpose, each other's reason for being. Now Erin was trying not to entertain ideas of losing Kevin this way, but somehow they still managed to find their way into her head. She curled up under her covers, still in her clothes, and cried herself to sleep.

39

As Kevin walked out of the gate, at the Vancouver airport, he saw Erin waiting anxiously for him. She smiled as soon as she saw him, barely able to wait for him to walk out. Beside her, Tory stood behind a stroller, with little Connor sleeping inside of it. Kevin smiled tiredly as he set his bag down to give hugs.

The last day and a half had passed slowly, with an additional day in Detroit for observation and assessment, a lengthy discharge process, and a long flight, the end of which was hard on Kevin's tender head. But the worst of his symptoms were reduced. His headaches came and went, rather than the sustained ache of two nights before. His vision was nearly back to normal, provided he didn't turn his head too quickly. And although splotchy in places, he had reassembled some of the events of the couple of days prior to his injury in his memory.

Erin held him cautiously, for several seconds, relieved to see that his faculties seemed to be restored. Kevin knelt down slowly to hug Tory. "Careful, Tory. Remember what Mommy said," Erin reminded Tory, who had a habit of throwing herself at her dad for her hugs. She stepped slowly towards him, nestling her head into his chest, and setting her hands gently on his shoulders. Kevin felt a little better instantly.

He wouldn't see the team physicians until the next day, giving him a chance to relax and be with his family. They spent the rest of the day together, taking turns tending to Connor. Tory entertained by reading a book, with some help, to her little brother, then singing him to sleep. He was a pretty easy baby, and Tory had had enough of a hand in his care that her voice seemed to sooth him. Kevin watched lovingly as he saw Erin's nurturing side in Tory. He felt truly happy, despite being bothered occasionally by dizzy spells.

That night, Kevin and Erin tucked Tory in together then went to bed. Erin fell asleep quickly, content that her family was safe and back to normal. It felt good to Kevin to lie in his own bed again, wishing that the difficult two nights in Detroit would vanish from his memory like the two nights prior to them had. But he was home now, and he felt much more himself.

Erin woke in the night, realizing that Kevin wasn't lying beside her. She looked in the bathroom, and he wasn't there. She felt a tightening in her stomach as she hurried downstairs to look for him. She saw him on the floor in the living room, curled up in a ball, rocking back and forth in the dark. His eyes were shut tightly, and his teeth clenched, fighting the pain in his head. Gordie circled him frantically, unable to help him.

Erin got down on her knees trying to stay calm. "Kev, are you okay?" He didn't respond. "Do you want me to take you to the hospital?" Still no reply. "Kev, I need you to tell me what you need me to do." Kevin finally opened his eyes and glanced up sideways at her, nodding slightly. "The hospital, Kev? Okay let me call Kate. Then we'll go."

Erin dialed Kate and Rick's number quickly, watching Kevin carefully. The voice on the other end sounded tired and confused. "Hello?"

"Kate, it's Erin. I need to take Kevin to the hospital. He 's in a lot of pain and I don't know what to do for him."

Kate gathered her senses quickly. "Okay, can you swing by here with the kids? I'll take care of them," she assured her.

"Thanks Kate. We'll be there in a bit." Erin hung up without saying goodbye, racing upstairs to gather up both kids. Connor cried all the way to the Olsens' house, disturbed by the quick wakening. Despite the crying, Kevin's headache appeared to be subsiding. By the time they'd dropped off the kids and the dog and arrived at the hospital, it had faded to a dull throb again. Erin held Kevin's hand tightly, trying to assure him that he would not be alone in this fight, whatever it entailed.

The physicians were conservative, insisting on an immediate CAT scan (computerized axial tomography) to assess the damage. The on-call neurologist finally came out to talk to them.

"Hi, Kevin. I'm Dr. Glasser. I'm the neurologist that ordered the CAT scan."

"Hi." Kevin responded, awaiting an explanation.

Glasser cut right to the chase, "You've had other concussions prior to this one, haven't you Kevin?"

Kevin nodded, "Yeah, I've had my share over the years, I guess."

Erin added to clarify, "This is his fifth in the last eighteen months or so, but I think there may have been others that weren't diagnosed."

"I think you're probably right," Glasser continued. "You see, Kevin, every time you have a concussion, your brain is bruised. Now I could see remnants of damage from previous hits in the pictures of your brain. However, there's no evident of what we call acute sub-dural bleeding or bleeding into the brain itself, which is good. But with your history of concussions and the subtle changes in your brain that are already detectable, each concussion that you sustain will cause greater damage." Erin held Kevin tightly around his shoulders as they listened. "The good news is: you've been pretty lucky so far. It doesn't sound like you've lost any major brain functioning. All the symptoms you described are pretty basic. The headaches, the blurred vision, short-term memory loss, they're usually temporary. The bad news is: it looks like you're probably just one good whack away from doing irreparable damage. I know this is hard to hear, Kevin, but that's the way it looks to me right now, and I've been doing this for a pretty long time. The other immediate good news is that it doesn't look like we'll have to intervene surgically at this point. The acute headache you had tonight was still aftermath of the last trauma, but does not appear to be the result of a decline in your condition. I'd like to admit you, just for a day or two for further observation. This isn't something we want to mess around with."

Both Erin and Kevin nodded in agreement. "Thank you, Dr. Glasser," Erin said appreciatively, shaking his hand before he left.

Kevin sat, staring at the floor, partly relieved that his headache had subsided, partly in shock from the news he'd just heard. Finally, he looked up at Erin and said quietly, almost matter-of-factly, "That's it, isn't it? I'm done."

Erin felt a piercing pain in her soul as he said it, knowing that he was probably right, feeling hopelessly unable to alter the reality that he was facing. "Let's just get you better first. Okay, sweetie?"

The next two days in the hospital were much more bearable, with frequent visits from Erin and Tory. They didn't bring Connor to the hospital, heeding warnings about infant susceptibility to infection. The two team physicians were in and out periodically, conferencing with Glasser when he was around.

Kevin was nearly symptom-free when he was released, with only faint headaches and bouts of dizziness that were comparable to the feeling of standing up too quickly. He went home, feeling relieved that his condition could be overcome, that he needn't be affected indefinitely by it.

40

Much to Kevin's surprise and Erin's dismay, the team doctors were approaching the situation with a wait-and-see attitude, reluctant to say one way or the other what the prognosis of Kevin's injury was. In the two weeks following his second hospital stay, Kevin was allowed to work out, lightly at first, then with greater intensity, even getting back on the ice for a few skates.

The team was now a week away from the playoffs, with a first round match-up with Detroit sealed mathematically. Marcel Boucher was growing increasingly impatient, awaiting the go-ahead from the team docs to let Kevin play. He had called a meeting between the coaching staff and the medical staff. Tony Paxton, although usually talkative, clcarly intended for the two physicians to do the talking. Jamie Harris sat uneasily on Boucher's desk, also saying nothing.

Boucher began, "We need an answer here, guys. When's he gonna be ready to go? He looks great on the ice. He says he feels fine. What are we waiting for here?"

Dr. Ben Hlady responded, "This isn't his first concussion, Marcel. Under the circumstances, he should be symptom free for at least a couple more weeks before we even think of letting him suit up again."

Boucher rolled his eyes in disgust, "Two more weeks?! He'd miss the first three games of the play-offs . . . again! You're gonna do that to him?"

Dr. Russell Townsend interjected, "You know, coach, we've got a neurosurgeon telling us not to let him dress again . . . ever. I think you'd be wise to accept our discretion on this one."

"Jesus Christ, Russell, this kid lives and breathes the game of hockey! What would he do without the game? Huh? What kind of life would he have?" The room was silent. "He's a hockey player, for Christ sake! You take that away from him and you might as well kill him!"

Harris squirmed as he listened, uncomfortable with Boucher's assumptions, even less comfortable with his own silence.

Boucher went on, "Well, ultimately, it's his decision, right?"

The two doctors nodded uneasily, then Russell Townsend spoke again, "He has to make the call, but we've got to give him honest advice."

"You're job is simple, Russell. You make your best guess of how long he needs, then tell him. Don't scare him. That'll just put him more at risk. I've seen a lot of players get a lot more concussions than he's had, that were just fine when they came back."

"It's not that simple, Marcel!" Ben Hlady shouted, losing patience.

"How long, gentlemen?" Boucher asked, looking away. They paused, longer than Boucher was willing to wait. "How long?!"

"*At least* a couple of weeks." Townsend said, disappointed in himself for not putting up more of a fight.

"Okay, tell him, and let him decide. That's all. Thank you."

Rick stood outside the closed door, looking through the glass at Harris, who looked back at him helplessly. He wondered why Boucher appeared to be doing more talking than anyone else, and why the team doctors looked so frustrated.

Harris was the first to leave, desperate to get out of the room where his own gut feeling was being trampled. Rick followed him down the corridor. "What'd they say, Bones?"

"At least two weeks, but they didn't seem convinced that that was enough either," Harris said, continuing to walk.

"Is there a big chance of him being damaged for good?" Rick asked, forcing the point.

"They didn't even talk about it. But I sure got the feeling that they thought so," Harris said, then he stopped in his tracks. "I've got a bad feeling about this, Olse. But what am I supposed to say? 'Bouche, I've got a bad feeling about this. Don't let him play'?"

Rick shrugged, "Well, hopefully the docs will level with him."

Minutes later, Kevin answered his cell phone, driving home from the rink. "Hello?"

"Hi Kevin, Russ Townsend here."

"Oh hey doc. What's the word?" Kevin asked, a little nervous as he waited.

"Well, we think you should be symptom-free for at least another couple of weeks before you suit up again." There was a pause before Townsend continued. "But you should also know that there's a certain amount of risk involved . . . but the organization wants you to have the ultimate say, Kevin. So you'd certainly be wise to talk it over with your neurologist."

So there it was. Kevin had been given the go ahead to play in two weeks. It seemed like encouraging news on the surface, but Kevin sensed that there was a subtext to Townsend's message. *Why would he mention the neurologist again? Why did he sound so uneasy? We've always had a comfortable relationship.* Kevin's thoughts raced as he turned into his driveway, bearing good news . . . that he knew would terrify Erin.

"Hi Sweetie!" Erin called from the kitchen when she heard the door. "Did you talk to the doctors today?" she asked, hoping that they would have made the decision for him, and made it based on caution.

"Yeah, just now. . . . They said I could go in a couple of weeks." Kevin said, shrugging.

Erin's face conveyed disapproval, fear, and a plea for reason simultaneously. "Kevin. This is crazy. You remember what Dr. Glasser said. How can you really be considering this?"

Kevin's face grew serious. "How can I be considering this? How about, 'because I've spent my whole life working towards this'? Or how about, 'because I don't have a friggin' clue what I'd do if I wasn't playing hockey'? You married a hockey player, Erin. I walk away now, and I stop being the man you fell in love with."

Erin's face tightened. She was ready for this fight, and she was not going to back down. "No Kevin! I married you because I loved *you*. Not Kevin Wilkins, the hockey player. Kevin, the person. Because you were thoughtful and caring. Because you were passionate and hard-working. Because you had a strength about you that made you beautiful." Kevin turned away, but Erin spun him back around. "Listen to me Kevin! You walk away now, and you need to redirect your focus, redirect your passion and your strength . . . and that will be tough. I'm not saying that it won't. But everything that I love most about you, you'll still have. And you'll also have a full life ahead of you, with a wife that loves you, and two beautiful children. But Kevin if you go back and play because you're afraid not to, then I'm afraid that maybe you will have lost the most important part of who you are."

Kevin stood with his arms crossed, unable to respond. Erin waited quietly for some sign that he understood what she had to say. Then the phone rang, startling them both. Kevin picked up quickly, welcoming the escape. "Hello?"

"Hi Kev, it's me, Brad."

Kevin sighed, knowing that Brad would be on the same wavelength as Erin. "Hey Brad, what's up?"

"I was just wondering what the word was from the team docs," Brad stated predictably.

"Good to go in two weeks," Kevin said, glancing at Erin, who stood, waiting impatiently to carry on their discussion.

Brad paused, "I kind of figured it would be something like that." He had retained a certain amount of cynicism about the power of the 'hockey business'. "Listen, Kev, I'm not gonna tell you how to live your life. I know you won't listen to a lecture from your little brother. But just hear me out for a second. If you're serious about coming back and playing after all that's happened, then you might as well get the best information that you can. Right?"

"Sure," Kevin answered, still feeling cornered.

"Okay. One of the guys from my thesis committee is best friends with a neurologist that works in Vancouver. And from the sounds of things, this guy is the foremost expert on head injuries on the continent. I talked to the guy that I know, and he was gonna put a call in for me, to let this guy in Vancouver know that you might call. If anyone would know whether you're at serious risk or not, Kev, from what I understand, this would be the guy. So all I'm asking is that you call him. Will you do that?"

Kevin's voice softened, giving in just this much. "Okay, you got a number?"

"Yep, you got a pen handy?"

"Yeah, go ahead," Kevin prompted.

"Okay, his name is Dr. Keith Glasser. His number is (604) 291-2535. Kev, you got that?"

Kevin dropped his pen and put his head back, closing his eyes. "That's the guy I saw already."

"Well, what did he tell you?" Brad asked hopefully.

Kevin sat down on a kitchen chair, completely deflated, suddenly feeling less trapped by his wife and brother than he was by a harsh reality that he finally had to face. Kevin's voice broke as he continued, "He said I was one hit away from permanent damage." Kevin tried to compose himself, taking deep breaths.

"Kev, . . . I'm sorry. I know this has got to be hard . . ." Brad responded awkwardly.

"You said it yourself, Brad! I'm nothing without hockey!" Kevin said in exasperation. Erin had positioned herself behind him, trying to hold him while he spoke.

Brad collected his thoughts quickly, "Kev, a lot has changed since then. You told me last summer that you finally knew what was most important in your life. And now you're still in a position to protect it. I know you a lot better now, Kev. You're a great dad. You saved your marriage and things are going great again. You're a great brother, a great friend. You're so much more than a hockey player, Kev. And the things that made you great in hockey will make you great in the next thing. I know it."

Kevin was now sobbing, faced with the decision that he knew was the right one. Tortured by its finality for the game that he'd poured himself into for years.

"Kev, I'm sorry you have to go through this. But I wouldn't tell you any of this if I didn't know that you've got so much more to live for. Just think about it, okay? I'll talk to you soon. Bye buddy."

Erin sat on Kevin's lap and held him, rocking from side to side. He cried for several minutes, clutching her tightly. He knew that Brad was right. He knew that Erin was right. But he needed to cry. He needed to feel the hurt of his loss if he was ever to recover from it.

That evening Kevin sat out on the bench in the back yard. The only noise was that of the crickets. The smell of the grass soothed him with each breath. He sought council from the stars, in particular, whichever one that Cormie was looking down from.

"Hey Cormie, me again. I feel like I'm falling here, and I'm not sure how to stop. I know my family is most important. And I love them with all my heart. But I want them to be proud of me. I want them to look up to me, to feel like there's something special about us. I feel like hockey gives me that. And now I'm about to lose it. I need some answers here, Cormie. What do I do now?"

Kevin waited patiently for his answer in the quiet. No response came. Then the door slid open. Tory maneuvered Connor's stroller out the door, careful not to tip it. Connor appeared unaffected by the jostling, seeming to take interest in the change in scenery. Tory pushed the stroller over to Kevin. "Connor wanted to say goodnight, before his story."

Kevin smiled, leaning down to kiss his son on the forehead. Then he did the same to Tory and patted her on the bum, as if to direct her back inside. He saw Erin standing inside, watching to ensure that Tory didn't have any trouble with her errand. When their eyes met, she smiled and mouthed the words 'I love you' for him to see. *Not a stick or a puck in sight. Maybe if I find a way to be proud, they'll be proud too*, he thought to himself. *Maybe what we have isn't based on pride at all.* "Thanks Cormie. You're the best," he whispered, as he stood to go back inside . . . maybe to catch a little bit of Connor's story.

41

Two days later. Eight Rinks Complex, Burnaby.

Kevin had called a 1pm press conference to make an announcement. He arrived at ten and got on the bike to warm up. He had asked Jamie Harris to arrange for him to get on the ice by himself, but asked that Vlad join him for a thirty minute skate. Harris decided that it would be fine for Vlad to have this skate with Kevin, in lieu of the team skate an hour later. That way, they could refine their timing again, before Kevin's return.

By 10:30, both players were on the ice, rocketing from end to end, passing back and forth, as if the puck was attached to both sticks by a string. They set each other up for one-timers. They threaded breakout passes to each other. They moved together in near perfect synchronicity, as if they were two skaters of the same mind. A few of the players arrived in time to catch the end of their exhibition, excited to see their two stars reunited. When they stepped off the ice, Kevin turned to Vlad and smiled. He took off his right glove and held out his hand. Vlad did the same in response, unsure of the occasion.

Then Kevin let him in on his secret. "It's been a pleasure playing with you, Vlad. Thanks." Vlad looked confused initially, then smiled back as he realized what had just happened. He nodded and replied, "The pleasure was mine."

Shortly before the press conference, Erin arrived with the kids. Kevin immediately felt more at ease. He sat with Harris, waiting for people to make their way into the conference room.

"So Bones, I've been dying to ask, why do they call you that?" Kevin asked, apparently unphased by the magnitude of the event.

"It's really not much of a story," Harris insisted.

"Come on, just tell me." Kevin prompted.

"Well, when I was in junior high, my dad and I used to watch Star Trek every week. One time he called me Bones, and it just kind of stuck." Harris explained sheepishly.

Kevin sat in silence for a moment, blinking a couple times in disbelief. "Are you kidding me?"

"No. That's it."

"I've waited this long to ask because I wanted you to have time to tell the whole story, and that's it?" Harris shrugged. "You've got to be kidding me."

Harris started to laugh. Kevin went on, "We call you Bones because you were a Trekky? Ah man. That's just sad. Well, the secret's safe with me. I couldn't break the other guys' hearts like that." The two shared a laugh that went on intermittently for the remainder of the time before the press conference.

It was time to start. Kevin walked shyly up onto the platform. Cameras snapped photos from the moment he sat down. Only a few of the media people dared to believe what they suspected about his announcement. He adjusted the microphone and began.

"Hi. Thanks for coming. I only wanted to do this once, that's why all the fuss. A few weeks ago, I sustained a concussion, the last of several that, as I understand, compromised my safety indefinitely. Under the advice of a renowned neurologist, with the support of my wife, Erin, and my two children, Tory and Connor, I have decided to retire from professional hockey." The room began buzzing wildly. "I would like to thank the Vancouver Canucks organization, especially my teammates for the wonderful years here. I'd like to thank the fans for all their support. And I would like to wish my teammates the best of luck in the play-offs, and in all of their future endeavours, both on and off the ice. I'd especially like to thank my linemates, Billy and Vlad, and our Captain . . ." Kevin's fight against his tears came to an end when he saw Rick at the back of the room, also welling up. "Rick . . . you stood by me all the way. My big brother and my friend . . . you'll always be my captain. Thanks for everything."

Kevin stepped down from the platform, ignoring the frenzy of questions from the media, embracing Erin and Tory at once, huddled together in solidarity. Then, one by one, his teammates came forward and either shook his hand or embraced him, and wished him well. When he and Rick hugged, Erin glanced up at a photographer who stepped forward to take a photo of the two of them together. Erin tapped the man on the shoulder and whispered, "I'm going to want a copy of that."

42

Eighteen years later.

A young man sat alone in the bleachers of the Red Deer Centrium, staring out at the pristine sheet of ice that would be the sight of tonight's game seven contest for the WHL championship. He appeared curiously at peace, for a player on which the series was thought to hinge. He began visualizing the game the way he intended to play it, taking slow, deep breaths as he conjured images in his head.

He then got up and walked slowly down to the dressing room, where his teammates had started their own preparations. He warmed up with a skipping rope. He played a hand-eye drill against the wall in the corridor with a tennis ball, by himself. He stretched out and then methodically donned his goalie gear. He pulled on his number 29 Portland Winterhawks jersey, with his name on the back: Wilkins.

Connor Wilkins had been the story in game 6 of the series, back in Portland. He had let in only 2 of 43 shots in the 3-2 victory, forcing a seventh game in Red Deer. As he sat, waiting for the on-ice warm-up, he reflected on the advice that his father had given him, that had always allowed him to relax and enjoy the games he was playing in. He needed it now more than ever, with the hype that the media had created about his dominating play. His name had come up repeatedly as a likely first round pick in the upcoming NHL draft.

But Connor's thoughts were simpler and truer to the game itself. He had an opportunity to play in a game seven, in the WHL final, where some of the finest young players in the world were assembled. He had an opportunity to influence the outcome significantly with his play. And he knew that his best chance to do that was to relax, savour the opportunity, . . . and just *play*. He smiled to himself as he marveled at the simplicity of his task, one that so many people choose to complicate: keep the puck out.

As the players completed their warm up, the stands began to fill. Two women made their way to their seats, both slim and attractive, one in her early twenties, the other in her early forties, but not showing her age. They sat down excitedly, then focused their attention on Connor, who was stopping shots at the other end, looking as sharp as ever.

"You think he's nervous, Mom?" Tory asked, as she bounced gently in her seat.

"He never seems to be, does he? But he probably is a little. You know, the 'good nervous' that your dad talks about," Erin replied.

"I think I'm nervous enough for both of them," Tory continued. "Eeeek!" she uttered anxiously, pressing her hands together, really more excited than nervous.

"Oh, there's Brad and Carla." The handsome couple walked briskly up to their seats beside Tory and Erin. The four traded hugs, then sat down.

"You were able to reschedule your afternoon clinic, Brad?" Erin asked.

"Yeah, Monday will be crazy as a result but . . . it's worth it." Brad said surely.

Down in the corridor, outside the Red Deer locker room, Kevin Wilkins paced back and forth slowly. His face showed a few lines of age, mostly smile lines, like the ones in the corners of Erin's eyes. He looked slender and fit, not as big as his playing days, but just as lean. And his dark hair was peppered with silver that made him look more distinguished.

He looked at his watch, then strolled slowly into the dressing room. "Okay, listen up, fellas."

His voice softened and he began. "These are the nights that dreams are made of. Game seven, Western League final. Jordan, when you sat on your tractor daydreaming in the summer, what were you thinking about?"

"This night." The player answered.

Kevin nodded, "This night. Yuri, on that long flight over from the Ukraine two years ago, what were you dreaming about?"

"This night." Another player answered, still with a thick accent.

"This night." Kevin nodded again. "Look around the room, fellas. Every one of you has gone through the wall for the team in these play-offs. You've got nothing left to prove. And it doesn't matter that you deserved to wrap this thing up in Portland. What matters is that we're here now, in front of our fans . . . living the dream. So savour it, boys. Soak up the environment. Feed off the electricity in the building. Because these nights come along once in a lifetime, for a fortunate few. Play smart. Play disciplined. Play together, and good things will happen. Marty's line, start us off with some contact. Let's go."

The room erupted and the players filed out into the corridor. The players of both teams walked up the ramps to their respective benches, piling onto the ice. Kevin stopped and looked down the hall. Connor stood at the other end, looking back. They both smiled and nodded at each other, then walked to the ice surface.

After the anthems, the crowd buzzed in anticipation. Connor pulled down his mask and moved side to side in his crease, working out the last of his nervous tension, then glided into position. Kevin stood behind the bench smiling, nudging his assistant coach in the shoulder to share the moment. The two forward lines glided to center, squaring off, waiting for the puck to be dropped.

EPILOGUE

During my graduate work, I had an opportunity to interview some of Canada's most remarkable athletes. What made them remarkable was not simply the level at which they were achieving (the group included professional athletes, international competitors, world & Olympic champions) but the fact that they all were regarded as *exceptional human beings*. I wanted to know why some athletes are contaminated by success, becoming disconnected from themselves and their core values, while others stay humble and grounded and, in so doing, they inspire and positively influence those around them. What I wanted to know was *how they lived*. What behaviours, beliefs, habits, philosophies, and factors protected them from the pressures of the high performance environment and the 'toxins of success'?

The transcripts from these interviews were a goldmine. I published two articles in the online *Journal of Excellence*, sharing their insights and experiences. But then it occurred to me; people are often most inspired and changed through story-telling. So I endeavoured to write a novel that would present these lessons in an entertaining, fictional format. Whether my effort was entertaining or not I leave to your judgment, but most of all I hope that the lessons woven into the story spoke to you with all the clarity and meaning of the conversations I carried on with these inspiring individuals.

The interviews revealed a process that I termed 'perspective'. This process is best described in the following way. Ideally we all want to be connected to ourselves and our environments in fulfilling ways, through the things we do, the people we're with, and the places where we spend our time. When successful, life has a rhythm and a vividness that feels right and is intensely rewarding. Our best chance of achieving this connection is to focus on the moment we're in, on each experience in and of itself, and to have cues for returning to it when we are distracted from it. Kevin Wilkins started out with a love of the game, a dedication to family, and a humble appreciation for his gifts and the people that helped to shape his talents.

But there are certain environmental hazards that can disconnect us from the purity of experience. One of these is the illusion that success will allow us to transcend our insecurities, that it will make us feel a greater sense of worthiness and belonging. And if we buy into this idea, we may become fixated on the 'implications' of our experiences rather than the experiences themselves. Rather than enjoying a three-way play with Billy and Vlad, Kevin may automatically tally goal totals in his head, noting that Vlad will receive more credit, more adulation, . . . more love.

It's a powerful illusion because when we are successful people *do* treat us differently. We *do* receive more positive attention. But the more astute individuals can see from inside the tornado that this attention is fickle and short-lived. What we crave is acceptance and a sense of true belonging; but the only thing that will *truly* satisfy this hunger is the knowledge that we ARE loved and accepted by key people, and that their love is NOT CONTINGENT UPON OUR SUCCESSES.

If you acknowledge that each of us has inherent value, that we are all unique and worthy of love, then the 'mirage' of success can lift. You can focus on the experience itself, on the power of experience for its own sake, not on the pot of gold it promises. Kevin's eyes were drawn away from the rainbow of experience by the bounty promised to the successful. It took a threat to those things of greatest value to him, his friend Cormie, his wife and daughter, to snap out of his state. And this is often the case; our eyes are drawn away from those things of most basic importance to us in favour of the sugary rewards of success, in spite of the 'nutritional deficit' that this creates. Tragically, we sometimes fail to see what is most important until we lose it. The fortunate ones realize in time to right the ship. Through patience, love and forgiveness from his loved ones, Kevin had this good fortune. On the other side of his sense of entitlement and preoccupation with stardom (fallout from his success), Erin found Kevin. Not Kevin Wilkins the NHL great, just Kevin . . . vibrant and whole. And through her grace and the help of an old friend, he found himself.